I0656965

D'Arcy Power

William Harvey

D'Arcy Power

William Harvey

ISBN/EAN: 9783337424756

Printed in Europe, USA, Canada, Australia, Japan

Cover: Foto ©Raphael Reischuk / pixelio.de

More available books at **www.hansebooks.com**

WILLIAM HARVEY

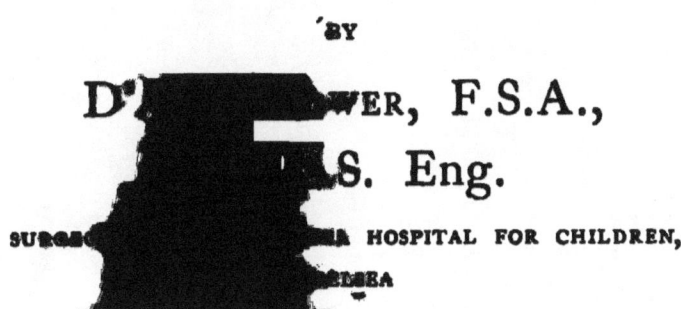

BY

D⁰ ⬛ER, F.S.A.,
⬛S. Eng.

SU⬛ ⬛ HOSPITAL FOR CHILDREN,
⬛LSEA

LONDON
FISHER UNWIN
⬛TERNOSTER SQUARE
MDCCCXCVII

*Copyright by T. Fisher Unwin, 1897, for Great Britain
and Longmans Green & Co. for the
United States of America*

To

DR. PHILIP HENRY PYE-SMITH, F.R.S.

IN RECOGNITION OF HIS PROFOUND KNOWLEDGE OF

THE PRINCIPLES ADVOCATED BY HARVEY, AND

IN GRATITUDE FOR MANY KINDNESSES

CONFERRED BY HIM UPON

THE AUTHOR

PREFACE

IT is not possible, nor have I attempted in this account of Harvey, to add much that is new. My endeavour has been to give a picture of the man and to explain in his own words, for they are always simple, racy, and untechnical, the discovery which has placed him in the forefront of the Masters of Medicine.

The kindness of Professor George Darwin, F.R.S., and of Professor Villari has introduced me to Professor Carlo Ferraris, the Rector Magnificus, and to Dr. Girardi, the Librarian of the University of Padua. These gentlemen, at my request, have examined afresh the records of the University, and have given me much information about Harvey's stay there. The Cambridge Archæological Society has laid me under an obligation by allowing me to reproduce the Stemma which still commemorates Harvey's official connection with the great Italian University. Dr. Norman Moore has read the proof sheets; his kindly criticism and accurate knowledge have added greatly to the value of the work, and he has lent me the block which illustrates the vileness of Harvey's handwriting.

I have collected in an Appendix a short list of authorities to each chapter that my statements may be verified, for Harvey himself would have been the first to cry out against such a gossiping life as that which Aubrey wrote of him.

D'ARCY POWER.

May 20, 1897.

CONTENTS

xi

WILLIAM HARVEY

I

HARVEY'S LINEAGE

THE history of the Harvey family begins with Thomas Harvey, father of William, the discoverer of the circulation of the blood. The careful search of interested and competent genealogists has ended in the barren statement that the family is apparently descended from, or is a branch of the same stock as, Sir Walter Hervey, "pepperer," or member of the ancient guild which afterwards became the important Company of Grocers. Sir Walter was Mayor of London in the year reckoned from the death of Henry III. in November, 1272. It was the noise of the citizens assembled in Westminster Hall clamouring for Hervey's election as Mayor that disturbed the King's deathbed.

The lineage would be a noble one if it could be established, for Hervey was no undistinguished Mayor. He was the worthy pupil and successor of Thomas Fitzthomas, one of the great champions in that struggle for liberty which ended in the death of Simon de Montfort, between Evesham and Alcester, but left the kingdom with a Parliament. Hervey's counsels reconstituted in London the system of civic government, and established it upon its present base ; for he assumed as chief of the executive the right to grant charters of incorporation to the craftsmen of the guilds. For a time his efforts were successful, and they wrought him much harm. But his idea survived, and in due season prevailed, for the companies have entirely replaced the guilds not only in London but throughout England.

It would be truly interesting if the first great discoverer in physiology could be shown to be a descendant of this original thinker on municipal government. The statement depends for the present on the fact that both bore for arms " argent, two bars nebulée sable, on a chief of the last three crosses pattée fitchée ; with the crest, a dexter hand appaumée proper, over it a crescent inverted argent," but arms were as often assumed in the reign of Elizabeth as they are in the Victorian era.

Thomas Harvey, the father of William, was born in 1549, and was one of a family of two brothers and three sisters, all of whom left children. Thomas married about 1575 Juliana, the eldest daughter of William Jenkin. His wife died in the following year, probably in childbed, for she left him a daughter, Julian or Gillian, who married Thomas Cullen, of Dover, and died about 1639.

Thomas Harvey married again on the 21st of January, 1576–77, his second wife being Joane, the daughter of Thomas Halke, or Hawke, who was perhaps a relative of his first wife on her mother's side. She lived at Hastingleigh, a village about six miles from Ashford in Kent, and to this couple William was born on the 1st of April, 1578, his father being then twenty-nine and his mother twenty-three.

William proved to be the eldest of "a week of sons," as Fuller quaintly expresses it, "whereof this William was bred to learning, his other brethren being bound apprentices in London, and all at last ended in effect in merchants." This statement is not strictly true, as only five of the sons became Turkey merchants and there were besides two daughters.

Thomas Harvey was a jurat, or alderman, of Folkestone, where he served the office of mayor in 1600. He lived in a fair stone house, which afterwards became the posthouse. Its site, however, is no longer known, though it is the opinion of those best qualified to judge that it stood at the junction of Church Street with Rendezvous Street.

Thomas Harvey seems to have been a man of more than ordinary intelligence and judgment, for " his sons, who revered, consulted, and implicitly trusted him, made their father the treasurer of their wealth when they got great estates, who, being as skilful to purchase land," says Fuller, " as they to gain money kept, employed and improved their gainings to their great advantage, so that he survived to see the meanest of them of far greater estate than himself." To this end he came to London after the death of his wife in 1605, and lived for some time at Hackney, where he died and was buried in June, 1623. His portrait is still to be seen in the central panel in one end wall of the dining-room at Rolls Park, Chigwell, in Essex, which was one of the first estates acquired by his son Eliab. " It is certainly," says Dr. Willis, " of the time when he lived, and it bears a certain resemblance to some of the likenesses we have of his most distinguished son."

All that is known of Joan Harvey is on a brass

tablet, which still exists to her memory in the parish church at Folkestone. It bears the following record of her virtues, written either by her husband or by William Harvey, her son :—

> "A.D. 1605 Nov. 8th died in the 50th. yeare of her age
> Joan Wife of Tho. Harvey. Mother of 7 sones & 2 Daughters.
> A Godly harmles Woman : A chaste loveinge Wife :
> A Charitable qviet Neighbour : A cōfortable frendly Matron :
> A provident diligent Hvswyfe : A carefvll tēder-harted Mother.
> Deere to her Hvsband : Reverensed of her Children :
> Beloved of her Neighbovrs : Elected of God.
> Whose Soule rest in Heaven, her body in this Grave :
> To her a Happy Advantage : to Hers an Unhappy Loss."

The children of Thomas and Joan Harvey were—

(1) William, born at Folkestone on the 1st of April, 1578; died at Roehampton, in Surrey, on the 3rd of June, 1657; buried in the "outer vault" of the Harvey Chapel at Hempstead, in Essex.

(2) Sarah, born at Folkestone on the 5th of May, 1580, and died there on the 18th of June, 1591.

(3) John, born at Folkestone on the 12th of November, 1582; servant-in-ordinary, or footman, to James I.—"a post," says Sir James Paget, "which does not certainly imply that he was in a much lower rank than his brothers. It may have been such a place at Court as is now called by a synonym of more seeming dignity ; or, if not, yet he may have received

a good salary for the office whilst he discharged its duties by deputy." Thus Burke in his famous speech on Economical Reform mentions that the king's *turnspit* was a member of Parliament.

He received a pension of fifty pounds a year when he resigned his place to Toby Johnson on the 6th of July, 1620. He was a member of Gray's Inn, and filled several offices of importance, for he was "Castleman" at Sandgate, in Kent, and King's Receiver for Lincolnshire jointly with his brother Daniel. He sat in Parliament as a member for Hythe, and died unmarried on the 20th of July, 1645.

(4) Thomas was born at Folkestone on the 17th of January, 1584–5. He married first Elizabeth Exton, about 1613; and, secondly, Elizabeth Parkhurst, on the 10th of May, 1621, and he had children by both marriages. His only surviving son sat as M.P. for Hythe in 1621; he also acted as King's Receiver for Lincolnshire. Thomas Harvey was a Turkey merchant in St. Laurence Pountney, at the foot of London Bridge. He was perhaps a member of the Grocers' Company. He died on the 2nd of February, 1622–3, and was buried in St. Peter-le-Poor.

(5) Daniel, also of Laurence Pountney Hill, a Turkey merchant and member of the Grocers' Com-

pany, was born at Folkestone on the 31st of May, 1587. He was King's Receiver for Lincolnshire jointly with his brother John. He married Elizabeth Kynnersley about 1619, paid a fine rather than serve the office of Sheriff of London at some time before 1640, and died on the 10th of September, 1649. He was a churchwarden of St. Laurence Pountney in 1624–5, and was buried there ; but his later days were spent on his estate at Combe, near Croydon, in Surrey. His fourth son became Sir Daniel Harvey, and was ambassador at Constantinople, where he died in 1672. His daughter Elizabeth married Heneage Finch, the first Earl of Nottingham, and from this marriage are descended the Earls of Winchelsea and Aylesford.

(6) Eliab, also of Laurence Pountney Hill, a Turkey merchant and member of the Grocers' Company, was born at Folkestone on the 26th of February, 1589–90. He was the most successful of the merchant brothers, and to his watchful care William owed much of his material wealth ; for Aubrey says that " William Harvey took no manner of care about his worldly concerns, but his brother Eliab, who was a very wise and prudent manager, ordered all not only faithfully but better than he could have done for himself." Eliab had estates at Roehampton, in Surrey,

7

and at Chigwell, in Essex. He built the "Harvey Mortuary Chapel with the outer vault below it" in Hempstead Church, near Saffron Walden. Here he buried his brother William in 1657, and here he was himself buried in 1661. He married Mary West on the 15th of February, 1624–5, and by her had several children, of whom the eldest at the Restoration became Sir Eliab Harvey.

Walpole writes to Mann about one of his descendants. "Feb. 6, 1780. Within this week there has been a cast at hazard at the Cocoa Tree, the difference of which amounted to an hundred and fourscore thousand pounds. Mr. O'Birne, an Irish gamester, had won £100,000 of a young Mr. Harvey of Chigwell, just started for a midshipman into an estate by his elder brother's death. O'Birne said, 'You can never pay me.' 'I can,' said the youth; 'my estate will sell for the debt.' 'No,' said O'B., 'I will win ten thousand—you shall throw for the odd ninety.' They did, and Harvey won." This midshipman afterwards became Sir Eliab Harvey, G.C.B., in command of the *Téméraire* at the battle of Trafalgar, and Admiral of the Blue. He sat in the House of Commons for the town of Maldon from 1780 to 1784, and for the county of Essex from 1802 until his death in 1830.

With him the male line of the family of Harvey became extinct.

(7) Michael, the twin brother of Matthew, was born at Folkestone on the 25th of September, 1593. He lived in St. Laurence Pountney, and St. Helen's, Bishopsgate. Like his other brothers he was a Turkey merchant, and perhaps a member of the Grocers' Company. He married Mary Baker on the 29th of April, 1630, and after her death Mary Millish, about 1635. He had three children by his second wife, and one of his sons died at Bridport in 1685 from wounds received in the service of King James II. Michael Harvey died on the 22nd of January, 1642–3, and is buried in the church of Great St. Helen's, Bishopsgate.

(8) Matthew, the twin brother of Michael, and like him a Turkey merchant and perhaps a member of the Grocers' Company, was born at Folkestone on the 25th of September, 1593. He married Mary Hatley on the 15th of December, 1628, and dying on the 21st of December, 1642, was buried at Croydon. His only child died in her infancy.

(9) Amye, the youngest daughter and last child of Thomas and Joan Harvey, was born at Folkestone on the 26th of December, 1596. She married George

Fowke in 1615, and died, leaving issue, at some time after 1645.

Mr. W. Fleming, the assistant librarian, tells me that nine autotype reproductions of the portraits of the Harvey family at Rolls Park (page 4) are now suspended on the left-hand side wall of the hall of the Royal College of Physicians in Pall Mall. They represent (1) Thomas Harvey and his seven sons. (2) William Harvey, probably an enlarged portrait of that in the preceding group. (3) A family group in the dress of the Queen Anne period. (4) Portrait of a lady in the dress of the reign of Queen Elizabeth ; in the corner of the picture appears "obiit 25 Maii 1622." (5), (6) and (7) Portraits of ladies in the dress of the eighteenth century. (8) Portrait of a gentleman in the dress of Charles II.'s time. (9) Portrait of a gentleman in the dress of Queen Anne's reign.

Early Life

VERY little is known of the early life of William
Harvey. His preliminary education was probably carried on in Folkestone, where he learnt the
rudiments of knowledge, gaining his first acquaintance
with Latin. One of his earliest distinct recollections
must have been in the memorable days in July, 1588,
when all was bustle and commotion in his native
town. The duty of resisting the Spanish Armada
in Kent and Sussex fell upon the " Broderield," or
confederation of the Cinque Ports, a body which
consisted of the Mayor, two elected Jurats, and two
elected Commoners from Hastings, Sandwich, Dover,
Romney, Hythe, Winchelsea, and Rye. And as
Folkestone for all purposes of defence was intimately
allied with Dover, it is not at all unlikely that Thomas
Harvey, one of its Jurats, was of its number, or that

he was a member of the " Guestling," which, affiliated
with the Broderield, had to fix the number, species,
and tonnage of the shipping to be found by each port,
a somewhat difficult task, as each port's share was a
movable quantity requiring constant rearrangement.
But even with the machinery of the Broderield and
the Guestling, it must have needed much activity to
raise the £43,000 which the Cinque Ports contributed
to set out the handy little squadron of thirteen sail
which did its duty under the orders of Lord Henry
Seymour in dispersing the remains of the great Spanish
fleet. Harvey must have had some remembrance of
the turmoil of the period, though it may have been
partially effaced by his new experiences at the King's
School, Canterbury, where he was entered for the first
time in the same year.

He remained at the King's School for five years, no
doubt coming home for the holidays, some of which
must have been spent in watching the constant trans-
port of troops to Spain and Portugal which was•so
noticeable a feature in the history of the Cinque Ports
during the later years of the life of Elizabeth.

His schooling ended, Harvey entered at once as
a pensioner, or ordinary student, at Caius College,
Cambridge, his surety being George Estey. The

record of his entry still exists in the books of the College. It runs: "Gul. Harvey, Filius Thomae Harvey, Yeoman Cantianus, ex oppido Folkeston, educatus in Ludo Literario Cantuar. natus annos 16, admissus pensionarius minor in commeatum scholarium, ultimo die Mai 1593." (William Harvey, the son of Thomas Harvey, a yeoman of Kent, of the town of Folkestone, educated at the Canterbury Grammar School, aged 16 years, was admitted a lesser pensioner at the scholars' table on the last day of May, 1593.)

The choice of the college seems to show that Harvey was already destined by his father to follow the medical profession. His habits of minute observation, his fondness for dissection and his love of comparative anatomy had probably shown the bias of his mind from his earliest years. Thirty-six years before Harvey's entry, Gonville Hall had been refounded as Gonville and Caius College, Cambridge, by Dr. Caius, who was long its master. Caius, in addition to his knowledge of Greek, may be said to have introduced the study of practical anatomy into England. His influence obtained for the college the grant of a charter in the sixth year of the reign of Queen Elizabeth, a charter by which the Master and Fellows were allowed to take annually the bodies of two criminals condemned to death and executed in Cambridge or its Castle free of all charges, to be used for the purposes of dissection, with a view to the increase of the knowledge of medicine and to benefit the health of her Majesty's lieges, without interference on the part of any of her officials. Unfortunately no record has been kept as to the use which the college made of this privilege, nor are there any means of ascertaining whether Harvey did more than follow the ordinary course pursued by students until he graduated as a Bachelor of Arts in 1597. His education, in all probability, had been wholly general thus far, consisting of a sound knowledge of Greek, a very thorough acquaintance with Latin, and some learning in dialectics and physics. He was now to begin his more strictly professional studies, and the year after he had taken his Arts degree at Cambridge found him travelling through France and Germany towards Italy, where he was to study the sciences more nearly akin to medicine, as well as medicine itself.

The great North Italian Universities of Bologna, Padua, Pisa, and Pavia, were then at the height of their renown as centres of mathematics, law, and medicine. Harvey chose to attach himself to Padua, and many reasons probably influenced him in his choice. The University was specially renowned for its anatomical school, rendered famous by the labours of Vesalius, the first and greatest of modern anatomists, and by the work of his successor, Fabricius, born at Aquapendente in 1537. Caius had lectured on Greek in Padua, and some connection between his college at Cambridge and his old University may still have been maintained, though it was now nearly a quarter of a century since his death. The fame of Fabricius and his school was no doubt the chief reason which led Harvey to Padua, but there was an additional reason which led his friends to concur cheerfully in his resolve. Padua was the University town of Venice, and the tolerance which it enjoyed under the protection of the great commercial republic rendered it a much safer place of residence for a Protestant than any of the German Universities, or even than its fellows in Italy. The matriculation registers which have recently been published show how large a number of its medical and law students were drawn from England and the other Protestant countries of Europe, and the English and Scotch " nation " existed in Padua as late as 1738, when the days of mediæval cosmopolitanism were elsewhere rapidly passing away.

The Universities of Europe have always been of two

types, the one Magistral, like that of Paris, with which we are best acquainted, for Oxford and Cambridge are modelled on Paris, and the Masters of Arts form the ruling body; the other, the Student Universities, under the control of the undergraduates, of which Bologna was the mother. Hitherto Harvey had been a member of a Magistral University, now he became attached to a University of Students, for Padua was an offshoot of Bologna. Hitherto he had received a general education mainly directed by the Church, now he was to follow a special course of instruction mainly directed by the students themselves, for they had the power of electing their own teachers, and in these points lies the great difference between a University of Masters and a University of Students.

In 1592 there were at Padua two Universities, that of the jurists, and that of the humanists—the Universitas juristarum and the Universitas artistarum. The jurists' University was the most important, both in numbers and in the rank of its students; the artistarum Universitas consisted of the faculties of divinity, medicine, and philosophy. It was the poorer, and in some points it was actually under the control of the jurists. In each university the students were enrolled according to their nationality into a series of " nations."

Each nation had the power of electing one, and in some cases two, representatives — conciliarii — who formed with the Rectors the executive of the University. The conciliarii, with the consent of one Rector, had the power of convening the congregation or supreme governing body ot the University, which consisted ot all the students except those poor men who lived "at other's expense."

Harvey went to Padua in 1598, but it appears to be impossible to recover any documentary evidence of his matriculation, though it would be interesting to do so, as up to the end of the sixteenth century each entry in the register is accompanied by a note of some physical peculiarity as a means of identifying the student. Thus :—

"D. Henricus Screopeus, Anglus, cum naevo in manu sinistrâ, die nonâ Junii, 1593." [Mr. Henry Scrope, an Englishman, with a birthmark on his left hand (matriculated), 9 June, 1593.]

"Johannes Cookaeus, anglus, cum cicatrice in articullo medii digiti die dicta." [John Cook, an Englishman, with a scar over the joint of his middle finger (matriculated) on the same day (9 June, 1593.] And at another time, "Josephus Listirus, anglus, cum parva cicatrice in palpebra dextera." [Joseph Lister, an

17   c

Englishman, with a little scar on his right eyebrow (matriculated on the 21st of November, 1598).]

Notwithstanding Harvey entered at Padua in 1598 no record of him has been found before the year 1600, although Professor Carlo Ferraris, the present Rector Magnificus and Dr. Girardi, the Librarian of the University, have, at my request, made a very thorough examination of the archives.

Dr. Andrich published in 1892 a very interesting account of the English and Scotch " nation " at Padua with a list of the various persons belonging to it. This register contains the entry, " D. Gulielmus Ameius, Anglus," the first in the list of the English students in the Jurist University of Padua for the new century as it heads the year 1600–1, and a similar entry occurs in 1601–2. There are also entries about this person which show that at the usual time of election, that is to say, on the 1st of August in the years 1600, 1601, and 1602, he was elected a member of the council (conciliarius) of the English nation in the Jurist University of Padua. His predecessors, colleagues, and successors in the council usually held office for two years. He was therefore either elected earlier into the council, or he was resident in the university for a somewhat longer time than the majority of the students.

Prof. Ferraris and Dr. Girardi have carefully examined this entry for me, and they assure me that there is no doubt that in the original the word is Arveius and not Ameius and that it refers to William Harvey. They are confirmed in this idea by the discovery of his "Stemma" as a councillor of the English nation for the year 1600. Stemmata are certain tablets erected in the university cloisters and in the hall or "Aula Magna" (which is on the first floor) to commemorate the residence in Padua of many doctors, professors, and students. They are sometimes armorial and sometimes symbolical. In 1892 Professor George Darwin carried an address from the University of Cambridge to that of Padua on the occasion of the tercentenary celebration of the appointment of Galileo to a Professorship in Padua. Professor Darwin then made a careful examination of these monuments so far as they related to Cambridge men, but he was unable to find any memorial of Harvey. Professor Ferraris continued the search, and on the 20th of March, 1893, he wrote to Professor Darwin : "We have succeeded in our search for the arms of Harvey. We have discovered two in the courtyard in the lower cloister. The first is a good deal decayed and the inscription has disappeared ; but the second is very well preserved and we have also discovered the inscription under a thin coating of whitewash which it was easy to remove." The monuments, which are symbolical, though Harvey was a gentleman of coat armour, are situated over the capitals of the columns in the concavity of the roof, one being in the left cloister, the other in the cloister opposite to the great gate of the court of the palace.

The kindness of Professor George Darwin has enabled me to reproduce this "stemma" from a photograph made for the Cambridge Antiquarian Society's publications. The memorial consists of an oval shield with a florid indented border having a head carved at each end of the oval. The shield shows a right arm which issues from the sinister side of the oval and holds a lighted candle round which two serpents are twined. Traces of the original colouring (a red ground, a white sleeved arm, and green serpents) remained on one of the monuments, and both have now been accurately restored by the Master and Fellows of Gonville and Caius College, Cambridge. A coloured drawing of the tablet has also been made at the expense of the Royal College of Physicians of London, and is now in their possession. A replica of this drawing was

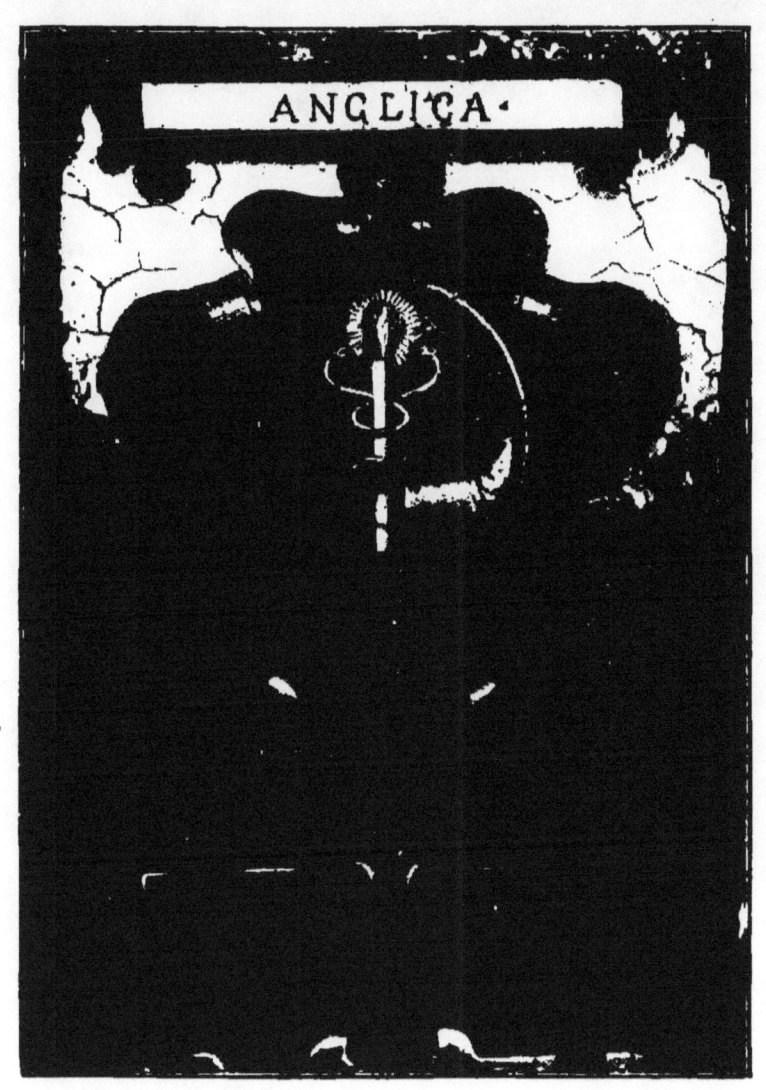

ANGLICA·

[To face page 20.

presented by the University Senate of Padua to Gonville and Caius College on the occasion of the dinner given in their hall in June, 1893, to commemorate the admission of Harvey to the college on the 31st of May, 1593.

It appears, therefore, that Harvey was a member of the more aristocratic Universitas Juristarum at Padua, which admitted a few medical and divinity students into its ranks, and that he early attained to the position of conciliarius of his nation. As a conciliarius Harvey must have taken part more than once in one of the most magnificent ceremonials which the university could show — the installation of a new Rector. The office of Rector was biennial, the electors being the past rectors, the councillors, and a great body of special delegates. The voting was by ballot, a Dominican priest acting as the returning officer. The ceremony took place in the Cathedral in the presence of the whole university. Here the Rector elect was solemnly invested with the rectorial hood by one of the doctors, and he was then escorted home in triumph by the whole body of students, who expected to be regaled with a banquet, or at the least with wine and spices. Originally a tilt or tournament was held, at which the new rector was required to provide two hundred spears and two hundred pairs of gloves; but this practice had been discontinued for some time before Harvey came into residence. A remarkable custom, however, remained, which allowed the students to tear the clothes from the back of the newly elected rector, who was then called upon to redeem the pieces at an exorbitant rate. So much license attended the ceremony that a statute was passed in 1552 to restrain "the too horrid and petulant mirth of these occasions," but it did not venture to abolish the time-honoured custom of the "vestium laceratio."

To make up for the magnificence of these scenes the Paduan student underwent great hardships. Food was scanty and bad, forms were rough, the windows were mere sheets of linen, which the landlord was bound to renew as occasion required; but to this Harvey was accustomed, for as late as 1598 the rooms of some of the junior fellows at King's College, Cambridge, were still unprovided with glass. Artificial ight was ruinously expensive, and there was an entire absence of any kind of amusement.

The medical session began on St. Luke's Day in each year, when there was an oration in praise of medicine followed by High Mass and the Litany of the Holy Ghost. The session lasted until the Feast of the Assumption, on August 15th, and in this time the whole human body was twice dissected in public by the professor of Anatomy. The greater part of the work in the university was done between six and eight o'clock in the morning, and some of the lectures were given at daybreak, though Fabricius lectured at the more reasonable hour (horâ tres de mane) which corresponded with nine o'clock before noon.

Hieronymus Fabricius was at once a surgeon, an anatomist, and the historian of medicine ; and as he was one of the most learned so he was one of the most honoured teachers of his day. Amongst the privileges which the Venetian Senate conferred upon the rector of the University of Padua was the right to wear a robe of purple and gold, whilst upon the resignation of his office he was granted the title for life of Doctor, and was presented with the golden collar of the Order of St. Mark. Fabricius, like the Rector, was honoured with these tokens of regard. He was granted precedence of all the other professors, and in his old age the State awarded him an annual pension of a thousand crowns as a reward for his services. The theatre in which he lectured still exists. It is now an ancient building with circular seats rising almost perpendicularly one above another. The seats are nearly black with age, and they give a most venerable appearance to the small apartment, which is wainscoted with curiously carved oak. The lectures must have been given by candlelight, for the building is so constructed that no daylight can be admitted. But when Harvey was at Padua the theatre was new, and the Government had placed an inscription over the entrance to commemorate the liberality as well as the genius of Fabricius, who had built the former theatre at his own expense. Here Harvey sat assiduously during his stay in Padua, learning charity, perhaps, as well as anatomy from his master ; for Fabricius had at home a cabinet set apart for the presents which he had received instead of fees, and over it he had placed the inscription, " Lucri neglecti lucrum."

Fabricius was more than a teacher to Harvey, for a fast friendship seems to have sprung up between master and pupil. Fabricius—then a man of sixty-one he lived to be eighty-two—was engaged during Harvey's residence in Padua in perfecting his knowledge of the valves of the veins. The valves had been known and described by Sylvius of Louvilly (1478–1555), that old miser, but prince of lecturers, who

warmed himself in the depth of a Parisian winter
by playing ball against the wall of his room rather
than be at the expense of a fire, and who threatened
to close the doors of his class-room until two defaulting
students either paid their fees or were expelled by their
fellows.   But the work of Sylvius had fallen into
oblivion and Fabricius rediscovered the valves in 1574.
His observations were not published until 1603, when
they appeared as a small treatise "de venarum ostiolis."
There is no doubt that he demonstrated their existence
to his class, and Harvey knew of the treatise, though
it was published a year after he had returned to
England.   Indeed, when we look at Harvey's work,
much of it appears to be a continuation and an
amplification of that done by Fabricius.   Both were
intensely interested in the phenomena of development;
both wrote upon the structure and functions of the
skin ; both studied the anatomy of the heart, lungs,
and blood vessels ; both wrote a treatise " de motu
locali."   Harvey's youth, his comparative freedom
from the trammels of authority, and his more logical
mind, enabled him to outstrip his master and to avoid
the errors into which he had fallen.   This advance
is particularly well seen in connection with the valves
of the veins.   Fabricius taught that their purpose

was to prevent over-distension of the vessels when the blood passed from the larger into the smaller veins (a double error) whilst they were not needed in the arteries because the blood was always in a state of ebb and flow. It was left for Harvey to point out their true use and to indicate their importance as an anatomical proof of the circulation of the blood.

Harvey graduated as Doctor of Medicine at Padua in 1602 in the presence, it is said, of Fortescue, Willoughby, Lister, Mounsell, Fox [disguised in the Records as Vulperinus], and Darcy, some of whom remained his friends throughout life. The eulogistic terms in which his diploma is couched leave no doubt that his abilities had made a deep impression upon the mind of his teachers. By some means it came into the hands of Dr. Osmond Beauvoir, head master of the King's School, Canterbury, by whom it was presented to the College of Physicians of London on September 30, 1766. The diploma is dated April 25, 1602, and it confers on Harvey the degree of Doctor of Physic, with leave to practise and to teach arts and medicine in every land and seat of learning. It further recites that "he had conducted himself so wonderfully well in the examination, and had shown such skill, memory, and learning that he had far surpassed even the great hopes which his examiners had formed of him. They decided therefore that he was skilful, expert, and most efficiently qualified both in arts and medicine, and to this they put their hands, unanimously, willingly, with complete agreement, and unhesitatingly."

Armed with so splendid a testimonial Harvey must have returned at once to England, for he obtained the degree of Doctor of Medicine from the University of Cambridge in the same year. The University records of Padua seemed to show that he maintained a somewhat close relationship with his Italian friends for some years afterwards as the following entries appear :—

" 1608–9 xxi. julii d. Gulielmus Herui, anglus.
ix-xxx d. Gulielmus Heruy.
30 D. Gulielmus Heruy anglus die xx aug. cons. anglicae electus."

The entries are given as they stand in Dr. Andrich's book, " De natione Anglica." They need further elucidation, for they either refer to some other person of the name of Harvey, or they point to visits made by Harvey in some of his numerous continental journeys. It is somewhat remarkable that all the records are found in the annals of the jurist university when Harvey should have belonged to the humanists. Perhaps the prestige of the dominant University more than compensated for the separation from his colleagues who were studying medicine. Indeed the separation may have been only nominal, for the students of the humanist and jurist universities might have sat side by side in the lecture theatre and in the dissecting room, just as members of the different colleges still do in Oxford. But party distinctions ran high at the time, and there was probably no more social intercourse between the members of the two universities than there is now between the individuals of different corps in a German university.

Soon after his return to England Harvey seems to have taken a house in London, in the parish of St. Martin's, extra Ludgate, and he lost no time in attaching himself to the College of Physicians. This body had the sole right of licensing physicians to practise in London and within seven miles of the City. Admission to the College was practically confined to graduates in medicine of the English Universities, but those who held a diploma from a foreign university were allowed to enrol themselves if they produced letters testimonial of admission *ad eundem* at Oxford or Cambridge, and perhaps it was for this reason that Harvey proceeded to qualify himself by taking his M.D. degree at Cambridge. He was admitted a Candidate of the College of Physicians on October 5, 1604, in the stone house, once Linacre's, in Knightrider Street, the candidates being the members or commonalty of the College from whom its Fellows were chosen.

Harvey married a few weeks after his admission to the College of Physicians. The Registers of St. Sepulchre's Church are wanting at this time, but the allegation for his marriage licence is still extant. It was issued by the Bishop of London and runs :—

1604 Nov. 24. William Harvey, Dr. of Physic, Bachelor, 26, of St. Martin's, Ludgate, and Elizabeth Browne, Maiden, 24, of St. Sepulchre's, daughter of Lancelot Browne of same, Dr. of Physic who consents ; consent also of Thomas Harvey, one of the Jurats of the town of Folston in Kent, father of the said William ; at St. Sepulchre's Newgate."

Dr. Browne was physician to Queen Elizabeth and to James I. He died the year following the marriage of his daughter.

Harvey's union was childless, and we know nothing of Mrs. Harvey except that she died before her husband, though she was alive in 1645, when John Harvey died and left her a hundred pounds. She is

incidentally mentioned by her husband in the following account of an accomplished parrot, who was Mrs.
Harvey's pet. Through a long life the parrot maintained the masculine character until in one unguarded
moment she lost both life and reputation.

" A parrot, a handsome bird and a famous talker,
had long been a pet of my wife's. It was so tame
that it wandered freely through the house, called for
its mistress when she was abroad, greeted her cheerfully when it found her, answered her call, flew to her,
and aiding himself with beak and claws, climbed up
her dress to her shoulder, whence it walked down her
arm and often settled upon her hand. When ordered
to sing or talk, it did as it was bidden even at night
and in the dark. Playful and impudent, it would
often seat itself in my wife's lap to have its head
scratched and its back stroked, whilst a gentle movement of its wings and a soft murmur witnessed to the
pleasure of its soul. I believed all this to proceed
from its usual familiarity and love of being noticed,
for I always looked upon the creature as a male on
account of its skill in talking and singing (for amongst
birds the females rarely sing or challenge one another
by their notes, and the males alone solace their mates
by their tuneful warblings) . . . until . . . not long

30

after the caressings mentioned, the parrot, which had lived for so many years in health, fell sick, and by and by being seized with repeated attacks of convulsions, died, to our great sorrow, in its mistress's lap, where it had so often loved to lie. On making a post-mortem examination to discover the cause of death I found an almost complete egg in its oviduct, but it was addled."

There are no means of knowing how Harvey spent the first few years of his married life in London, though it is certain that he was not idle. He was probably occupied in making those observations on the heart and blood vessels which have since rendered his name famous. Indeed his lectures show an intimate acquaintance with the anatomy of more than sixty kinds of animals, as well as a very thorough knowledge of the structure of the human body, and such knowledge must have cost him years of patient study. At the same time he practised his profession, and won for himself the good opinion of his seniors.

He was elected a Fellow of the College of Physicians, June 5, 1607, and thereupon he sought almost immediately to attach himself to St. Bartholomew's Hospital.

The offices in the hospital at that time were usually granted in reversion—that is to say, a successor was appointed whilst the occupant was still in possession. Following this custom the hospital minutes record that—

"At a Court [of Governors] held on Sunday, the 25th day of February, Anno Domini 1608–9,

"In presence of Sir John Spencer, Knight, President (and others).

"Mr.[1] Dr. HARVEY

"This day Mr. William Harvey Doctor of Physic made suit for the reversion of the office of the Physician of this house when the same shall be next void and brought the King's Majesty his letters directed to the Governors of this house in his behalf, and showed forth a testimony of his sufficiency for the same place under the hand of Mr. Doctor Adkynson president of the College of the physicians and diverse other doctors of the auncientest of the said College. It is granted at the contemplation of his Majesty's letters that the said Mr. Harvey shall have the said office next after the decease or other departure of

---

[1] The usual contraction for Magister, indicating his university degree of Artium Magister or M.A.

Mr. Doctor Wilkenson who now holdeth the same with the yearly fee and duties thereunto belonging, so that then he be not found to be otherwise employed, that may let or hinder the charge of the same office, which belongeth thereunto."

This grant practically gave Harvey the position which is now occupied by an assistant physician, as one who was appointed to succeed to an office in this manner was usually called upon to discharge its duties during the absence or illness of the actual holder. Harvey seems to have carried out his duties with tact and zeal, for Dr. Wilkinson, himself a Fellow of Trinity College, Cambridge, gave him the benefit of his professional experience and remained his friend.

It seems possible that John Harvey's position at Court enabled him to obtain from the King the letters recommendatory which rendered his brother's application so successful at St. Bartholomew's Hospital. However this may be, Harvey did not long occupy the subordinate position, for Dr. Wilkinson died late in the summer of 1609, and on August 28 in the same year Harvey offered himself to the House Committee " to execute the office of physician of this house until Michaelmas next, without any recompense for his pains herein, which office Mr. Doctor Wilkinson, late deceased, held. And Mr. Doctor Harvey being asked whether he is not otherwise employed in any other place which may let or hinder the execution of the office of the physician toward the poor of this hospital hath answered that he is not, wherefore it is thought fit by the said governors that he supply the same office until the next Court (of governors). And then Mr. Doctor Harvey to be a suitor for his admittance to the said place according to a grant thereof to him heretofore made." The form of his election therefore was identical with that which is still followed at the Hospital in cases of an appointment to an uncontested vacancy. The House Committee or smaller body of Governors recommend to the whole body or Court of Governors with whom the actual appointment lies.

Harvey performed his duties as physician's substitute at the hospital until—

" At a Court [of Governors] held on Sunday the 14th day of October 1609.

" In presence of Sir John Spencer, Knight, President (and others).

" Dr. HARVEY.

" This day Mr. William Harvey Doctor of Physic

is admitted to the office of Physician of this Hospital, which Mr. Dr. Wilkenson, deceased, late held, according to a former grant made to him and the charge of the said office hath been read unto him."

The charge runs in the following words ; it is dated the day of Harvey's election :—

"*October* 14, 1609.

" The Charge of the Physician of St. Bartholomew's Hospital.

" PHYSICIAN.

" You are here elected and admitted to be the physician for the Poor of this Hospital, to perform the charge following, That is to say, one day in the week at the least through the year or oftener as need shall require you shall come to this hospital and cause the Hospitaller, Matron, or Porter to call before you in the hall of this hospital such and so many of the poor harboured in this hospital as shall need the counsell and advice of the physician. And you are here required and desired by us, in God his most holy name, that you endeavour yourself to do the best of your knowledge in the profession of physic to the poor then present, or any other of the poor at any time of the week which shall be sent home unto you by the

35

Hospitaller or Matron for your counsel, writing in a book appointed for that purpose such medicines with their compounds and necessaries as appertaineth to the apothecary or this house to be provided and made ready for to be ministered unto the poor, every one in particular according to his disease. You shall not, for favour, lucre, or gain, appoint or write anything for the poor but such good and wholesome things as you shall think with your best advice will do the poor good, without any affection or respect to be had to the apothecary. And you shall take no gift or reward ot any of the poor of this house for your counsel. This you will promise to do as you shall answer before God, and as it becometh a faithful physician, whom you chiefly ought to serve in this vocation, is by God called unto and for your negligence herein, if you fail, you shall render account. And so we require you faithfully to promise in God his most holy name to perform this your charge in the hearing of us, with your best endeavour as God shall enable you so long as you shall be physician to the poor of this hospital."

Dr. Norman Moore says that, as physician, Harvey sat once a week at a table in the hall of the hospital, and that the patients who were brought to him sat by his side on a settle—the apothecary, the steward, and the matron standing by whilst he wrote his prescriptions in a book which was always kept locked. The hall was pulled down about the year 1728, but its spacious fireplace is still remembered because, to maintain the fire in it, Henry III. granted a supply of wood from the Royal Forest at Windsor. The surgeons to the hospital discharged their duties in the wards, but the physician only went into them to visit such patients as were unable to walk.

The office of physician carried with it an official residence rented from the governors of the hospital at such a yearly rent and on such conditions as was agreed upon from time to time. Harvey never availed himself of this official residence, for at the time of his election he was living in Ludgate, where he was within easy reach of the hospital. For some reason, however, it was resolved at a Court of Governors, held under the presidency of Sir Thomas Lowe on July 28, 1614, that Harvey should have this residence, consisting of two houses and a garden in West Smithfield adjoining the hospital. The premises were let on lease at the time of the grant, but the tenure of Harvey or of his successor was to begin at its expiration. The lease did not fall in until 1626, when Harvey, after some consideration, decided not to accept it. It was therefore agreed, on July 7, 1626, that his annual stipend should be increased from £25 to £33 6s. 8d. In these negotiations, as well as in some monetary transactions which he had with the steward of the hospital at the time of his election as physician to the hospital, we seem to see the hand of Eliab, for throughout his life William was notoriously open-handed, indifferent to wealth, and constitutionally incapable of driving a bargain.

The Lumleian Lectures

UNTIL the year 1745 the teaching of Anatomy in England was vested in a few corporate bodies, and private teaching was discouraged in every possible way, even by fine and imprisonment. The College of Physicians and the Barber Surgeons' Company had a monopoly of the anatomical teaching in London. In the provinces the fragmentary records of the various guilds of Barber Surgeons show that many of them recognised the value of a knowledge of Anatomy as the foundation of medicine. In the universities there were special facilities for its teaching. But subjects were difficult to procure, and dissection came to be looked upon as part of a legal process so inseparably connected with the death penalty for crime that it was impossible to obtain even the body of a " stranger " for anatomical purposes.

The Act of Parliament which, in 1540, united the Guild of Surgeons with the Company of Barber Surgeons in London especially empowered the masters of the united company to take yearly the bodies of four malefactors who had been condemned and put to death for felony for their " further and better knowledge, instruction, insight, learning, and experience in the science and faculty of surgery." Queen Elizabeth, following this precedent, granted a similar permission to the College of Physicians in 1565. The Charter allowed the President of the College of Physicians to take one, two, three, or four bodies a year for dissection. The radius from which the supply might be obtained was enlarged, so that persons executed in London, Middlesex, or any county within sixteen miles might be taken by the college servants.

The proviso would appear to be unnecessary, considering the great number of executions which then took place and the small number of bodies which were required, but it probably enabled the subjects to be obtained with greater ease. The executions in London were witnessed by great crowds, who often sided with the friends of the felons, and rendered it impossible for the body to be taken away for dissection. The Charter of James I. enlarged these powers by allowing the College of Physicians to take annually the bodies of six felons executed in London, Middlesex, or Surrey.

Little is known in detail of the manner in which Anatomy was taught by the College of Physicians, but the labours of Mr. Young and Mr. South have given us an accurate picture of the way in which it was carried out by the Barber Surgeons in London. We may be sure that in so conservative an age the methods did not differ greatly at the two institutions, especially as the Barber Surgeons usually enlisted the services of the better trained physicians to teach their members both Anatomy and Surgery.

Anatomy was taught practically in a series of demonstrations upon the body ; but as there was no means of preserving the subject, it had to be taught by a general survey rather than in minute detail. The method adopted was the one still followed by the veterinary student. A single body was dissected to show the muscles (this was the muscular lecture) ; another to show the bones (the osteological lecture) ; another to show the parts within the head, chest, and abdomen (the visceral lecture). The osteological lecturer was not always identical with the visceral lecturer, nor he with the lecturer upon the muscles, though some great teachers, like Reid and Harvey, gave a course upon each subject.

The Demonstrations usually took place four times a year, and were called Public Anatomies, because the subject was generally a public body—that is to say, it was a felon executed for his misdeeds. There was also an indefinite number of Private Anatomies. The attendance of surgeons at the Public Anatomies was compulsory. The attendance at the Private Anatomies was by invitation. It was illegal for any surgeon to dissect a human body in the City of London, or within a radius of seven miles, without permission of the Barber Surgeons' Company ; and in 1573 the Company's Records for May 21st contain the minute : "Here was John Deane and appointed to bring in his fine of ten pounds (for having an Anatomy in his house contrary to an order in that behalf) between this and Midsummer next "— an enormously heavy punishment when we remember the relative value of money in those days. Whenever a surgeon wished to dissect a particularly interesting subject, it was termed a Private Anatomy, and it was generally performed at the Hall of the Company after due permission had been asked for and obtained, the surgeon inviting his own friends and pupils, the Company inviting whom it chose.

Every effort was made to insure the punctual attendance at the public or compulsory anatomies, for it was enacted in 1572 that every man of the Company using the mystery or faculty of surgery, be he freeman, foreigner, or alien stranger, shall come unto the Anatomy lecture, being by the beadle warned thereto. And for not keeping their hour, both in the forenoon and also in the afternoon, and being a freeman, shall forfeit and pay at every time fourpence. The foreigner (or one who was not free of the Company) in like manner, and the stranger sixpence. The said fines and forfeits to be employed by the anatomists for their expenses. Excuses were sometimes admitted, for a few years earlier Robert Mudsley " hath licence to be absent from all lecture days without payment of any fine because he hath given over exercising of the art of Surgery and doth occupy only a silk shop and shave." In later years, the higher the position of the defaulter in the Company, the heavier was his fine for non-attendance; so that the assistants of the Company, who corresponded to the Council of the present Royal College of Surgeons, were fined 3s. 4d. for each lecture they missed.

Every effort was made to render the lectures

successful. The best teachers were obtained ; they were paid liberally, and each lecturer or reader was himself assisted by two demonstrators. Each course lasted three days—a lecture in the morning, a lecture in the afternoon, and a feast between the two lectures. As the anatomies were a public show, we may feel sure that Pepys attended one, and, as usual, he gives a perfectly straightforward account of the proceedings. He records under the date February 27, 1662–3 : " Up and to my office. . . . About eleven o'clock Commissioner Pett and I walked to Chyrurgeon's Hall (we being all invited thither, and promised to dine there), where we were led into the Theatre : and by and by comes the reader Dr. Tearne, with the Master and Company in a very handsome manner : and all being settled, he begun his lecture, this being the second upon the kidneys, ureters, &c., which was very fine ; and his discourse being ended, we walked into the Hall, and there being great store of company, we had a fine dinner and good learned company, many Doctors of Phisique, and we used with extraordinary great respect. . . . After dinner Dr. Scarborough took some of his friends, and I went along with them, to see the body alone, which we did, which was a lusty fellow, a seaman that was hanged for a robbery.

I did touch the dead body with my bare hand : it felt cold, but methought it was a very unpleasant sight. . . . Thence we went into a private room, where I perceive they prepare the bodies, and there were the kidneys, ureters, &c., upon which he read to-day, and Dr. Scarborough, upon my desire and the company's, did show very clearly the manner of the disease of the stone and the cutting, and all other questions that I could think of. . . . Thence with great satisfaction to me back to the Company, where I heard good discourse, and so to the afternoon lecture upon the heart and lungs, &c., and that being done we broke up, took leave and back to the office, we two, Sir W. Batten, who dined here also, being gone before." Pepys' interest in this particular lecture lay in the fact that he had himself been cut for stone, a disease which seems to have been hereditary in his mother's family. Dr. Scarborough, who had been the Company's lecturer for nineteen years, was the friend and pupil of Harvey, whose interest had obtained the post for him. He seems to have been succeeded by Dr. Christopher Terne, assistant physician to St. Bartholomew's Hospital, whose lecture Pepys heard.

The cost of the lectures and demonstrations was

defrayed at first by the Corporations, but in course of time, benefactors came forward and bequeathed funds for the purpose. In the year 1579 there was a motion before the Court of the Barber Surgeons' Company concerning a lecture in surgery "to be had and made in our Hall and of an annuity of ten pounds to be given for the performance thereof yearly by Master Doctor Caldwall, Doctor in phisick ; but it was not concluded upon neither was any further speech at that time." No reference to the proposal occurs subsequently in the minute books, so that the idea was probably abandoned, no doubt upon the ground that it would lead to additional expense which the Company was unprepared to meet. The annuity was only ten pounds a year, and in 1646 the cost of the lectures, including the dinners, amounted to £22 14s. 6d., or without the feasts to £12 14s. 6d. It is now obvious that the Company did a very stupid thing, for in 1581, two years later, Lord Lumley in conjunction with Dr. Caldwell, and at his instance, founded the Lumleian lectureship at the College of Physicians. The surgeons thus lost a noble benefaction which should of right have belonged to them and with which Harvey might still have been associated, for whilst he

was lecturing at the College of Physicians, Alexander
Reid, his junior in years as well as in standing, was
lecturing at the Barber Surgeons' Hall in Monkwell
Street.

The Lumleian lecture was a surgery lecture established at a cost of forty pounds a year, laid as a
rent charge upon the lands of Lord Lumley in Essex,
and of Dr. Caldwell in Derbyshire.

Its founders were two notable men. Lord Lumley,
says Camden, was a person of entire virtue, integrity,
and innocence, and in his old age, was a complete
pattern of true nobility. His father, the sixth baron,
suffered death for high treason, but the son was made a
Knight of the Bath two days before the coronation of
Queen Mary. He was one of the lords appointed to
attend Queen Elizabeth at her accession, in the
journey from Hatfield to London, and at the
accession of James I. he was made one of the
Commissioners for settling the claims at his coronation. He died April 11, 1609, without surviving
issue. Dr. Caldwell had enjoyed unique honour at
the College of Physicians. He was examined,
approved, and admitted a Fellow upon 22nd
December, 1559, and upon the same day he was
appointed a Censor. He became President in

1570, and was present at the institution of the
lecture in 1582. He was then so aged, his white
head adding double reverence to his years, that when
he attempted to make a Latin oration to the auditors
he was compelled to leave it unfinished by reason of
his manifold debilities. And in a very short time
afterwards the good old doctor fell sick, and as a
candle goeth out of itself or a ripe apple falleth
from a tree, so departed he out of this world at the
Doctors' Commons, where his usual lodgings were, and
was buried on the 6th of June immediately following,
in the year 1584, at S. Ben'et's Church by Paul's
Wharf, at the upper end of the chancel.

The design of the benefaction was a noble one. It
was the institution of a lecture on Surgery to be
continued perpetually for the common benefit of
London and consequently of all England, the like
whereof had not been established in any University
of Christendom (Bologna and Padua excepted). An
attempt had been made to establish such a lectureship
at Paris, but the project failed when Francis I. died,
on the last day of March, 1547.

The reader of the Lumleian lecture was to be a
Doctor of Physic of good practice and knowledge
who was to be paid an honest stipend, no less in

amount than that received by the Regius Professors of law, divinity, and physic, in the Universities of Oxford and Cambridge. The lecturer was enjoined to lecture twice a week throughout the year, to wit on Wednesdays and Fridays, at ten of the clock till eleven. He was to read for three-quarters of an hour in Latin and the other quarter in English "wherein that shall be plainly declared for those that understand not Latin."

The lecturer was appointed for life and his subjects were so arranged that they recurred in cycles. The first year he was to read the tables of Horatius Morus, an epitome or brief handling of all the whole art of surgery, that is, of swellings, wounds, ulcers, bone-setting, and the healing of broken bones commonly called fractures. He was also to lecture upon certain prescribed works of Galen and Oribasius, and at the end of the year in winter he was directed "to dissect openly in the reading place all the body of man, especially the inward parts for five days together, as well before as after dinner ; if the bodies may last so long without annoy."

The second year he was to read somewhat more advanced works upon surgery and in the winter "to dissect the trunk only of the body, namely, from the head to the lowest part where the members are and to handle the muscles especially. The third year to read of wounds, and in winter to make public dissections of the head only. The fourth year to read of ulcers and to anatomise [or dissect] a leg and an arm for the knowledge of muscles, sinews, arteries, veins, gristles, ligaments, and tendons. The fifth year to read the sixth book of Paulus Aegineta, and in winter to make an anatomy of a skeleton and therewithall to show the use of certain instruments for the setting of bones. The sixth year to read Holerius of the matter of surgery as well as of the medicines for surgeons to use. And the seventh year to begin again and continue still."

The College of Physicians made every effort to fulfil its trust adequately. Linacre, its founder and first President in 1518, allowed the Fellows to use the front part of his house—the stone house in Knightrider Street, consisting of a parlour below and a chamber above, as a council room and library, and the college continued to use these rooms for some years after his death, the rest of the premises being the property of Merton College, Oxford. At the Institution of the Surgery lecture the Fellows determined to appropriate the sum of a hundred pounds out of their common stock—and this proved to be nearly all the money the College possessed—to enlarge the building and to make it more ornamental and better suited for their meetings and for the attendance at their lectures. The result appears to have been satisfactory, for two years later, it was ordered, on the 13th of March, 1583–4, that a capacious theatre should be added to the College thus enlarged.

Dr. Richard Forster was appointed the first Lumleian lecturer, and when he died in 1602, William Dunne took his place. Dunne, however, did not live to complete a single cycle of lectures for Thomas Davies was elected in May, 1607. The College then again began to outgrow its accommodation, and as the site did not allow of any further additions to the buildings, a suitable house and premises were bought of the Dean and Chapter of St. Paul's in Amen Corner, at the end of Paternoster Row. The last meeting of the College in Linacre's old house in Knightrider Street, took place on the 25th of June, 1614, and its first meeting in Amen Corner was held on the 23rd of August, 1614. Dr. Davies died in the following year, and on the 4th of August, 1615, William Harvey was appointed to the office of Lumleian lecturer, though his predecessor was not buried until August 20th. He continued to occupy this post until his resignation in 1656, when his place was taken by (Sir) Charles Scarborough. The duties of the lecturer, no doubt, had been modified with each fresh appointment, but even in Harvey's time, there is some evidence to show that the subjects were still considered in a definite order.

Harvey, in all probability, began to lecture at once upon surgery as the more theoretical portion of his subject, but it was not until April, 1616, that he gave his first anatomical lecture. It was a visceral lecture for the terms of the bequest required that it should be upon the inward parts. At this time Harvey was thirty-seven years of age. A man of the lowest stature, round faced, with a complexion like the wainscot; his eyes small, round, very black and full of spirit; his hair as black as a raven and curling; rapid in his utterance, choleric, given to gesture, and used when in discourse with any one, to play unconsciously with the handle of the small dagger he wore by his side.

The MS. notes of his first course of lectures are now in the British Museum. They formed a part of the library of Dr. (afterwards Sir Hans) Sloane, which was acquired under the terms of his will by the nation in 1754. For a time the book was well known and extracts were made from it, then it disappeared and for many years it was mourned as irretrievably lost. But in 1876 it was found again amongst some duplicate printed books which had been set aside, and in the following year it was restored to its place in the Manuscript Department. The notes were reproduced by an autotype process, at the instigation of Sir E. H. Sieveking, and under the supervision of a Committee of the Royal College of Physicians. This facsimile reproduction was published in 1886 with a transcript by Mr. Scott, and an interesting introduction from the pen of Dr. Norman Moore. The original notes are written upon both sides of about a hundred pages of foolscap, which had been reduced to a uniform size of six inches by eight, though the creases on the paper show that they have been further folded so as to occupy a space of about eight inches by two. These leaves have been carefully bound together in leather which presents some pretensions to elegance, but it is clear that the pages were left loose for some years after they were written. There seems to be no doubt that Harvey used the volume in its present form whilst he was lecturing, for three small threads of twine have been attached by sealing wax to the inner side of the cover so that additional notes could be slipped in as they were required. It must be assumed that Harvey did this himself, for he wrote so badly and the notes are so full of abbreviations, interlineations, and alterations, as to render them useless to any one but the author.

The title-page, which is almost illegible, is written in red ink. It runs, "Stat Jove principium, Musae, Jovis omnia plena. Prelectiones Anatomiae Universalis per me Gulielmum Harveium Medicum Londinensem Anatomie et Chirurgie Professorem. Anno Domini 1616. Anno aetatis 37 prelectae Aprili 16, 17, 18. Aristoteles Historia Animalium, lib. i. cap. 16. Hominum partes interiores incertae et incognitae quam ob rem ad caeterorum Animalium partes quarum similes humanae referentes eas contemplare." The motto prefixed to the title-page that "everything is full of Jove" is an incorrect quotation from the third Eclogue of his favourite author Virgil, of whom he was so enamoured that after reading him for a time he would throw away the book with the exclamation, "He hath a devil." This particular line appears especially to have struck his fancy, for he quotes it twice in his treatise on development, and he works out the idea which it represents in his fifty-fourth essay.

He there shows that he understands it to mean that the finger of God or nature, for with him they are synonymous terms, is manifest in every detail of our structure whether great or small. For he says : " And to none can these attributes be referred save to the Almighty, first cause of all things by whatever this name has been designated—the Divine Mind by Aristotle ; the Soul of the Universe by Plato ; the Natura Naturans by others ; Saturn and Jove by the Gentiles ; by ourselves, as is seemly in these days, the Creator and Father of all that is in heaven and earth, on whom all things depend for their being, and at whose will and pleasure all things are and were engendered." He thus opened his lectures in a broad spirit of religious charity quite foreign to his environment but befitting the position he has been called upon to occupy in the history of science.

These notes of Harvey's visceral lecture are of especial value to us though they are a mere skeleton of the course—a skeleton which he was accustomed to clothe with facts drawn from his own vast stores of observation, with the theories of all his great predecessors and with the most apposite illustrations. Fortunately they deal with the thorax and its contents so that they show us the exact point which he had reached in connection with his great discovery of the circulation of the blood and the true function of the heart. The notes therefore are interesting reading quite apart from the peculiarities of their style.

Harvey was so good a Latin scholar, and during his stay in Italy had acquired such a perfect colloquial knowledge of the language that it is clear he thought with equal facility in Latin or in English, so that it is immaterial into which language he put his ideas. He uses therefore many abbreviations, and whole sentences are written in a mixture of Latin and English, which always sounds oddly to our unaccustomed ears, and often seems comical. Thus, in speaking of the lungs and their functions, he says, "Soe curst children by eager crying grow black and suffocated *non deficiente animali facultate*," and in speaking of the eyes and their uses, he says, " Oculi eodem loco, viz., Nobilissimi supra et ante ad processus eminentes instar capitis in a Lobster . . . snayles cornubus tactu pro visu utuntur unde occuli as a Centinell to the Army locis editis anterioribus." Sometimes he embodies an important experimental observation in this jargon as in the example, " Exempto corde, frogg scipp, eele crawle, dogg Ambulat."

The more important and original ideas throughout

the notes are initialled WH., and this seems to have been Harvey's constant practice, for it occurs even in the books which he has read and annotated, whilst to other parts of his notes he has appended the sign Δ.

The lectures were partly read and partly oral, and we know from the minute directions laid down by the Barber Surgeons Company the exact manner in which they were given. The "Manual of Anatomy," published by Alexander Reid in 1634, has a frontispiece showing that the method of lecturing adopted in England was the same as that in use throughout Europe. The body lay upon a table, and as the dissections were done in sight of the audience, the dissecting instruments were close to it. The lecturer, wearing the cap of his doctor's degree, sate opposite the centre of the table holding in his hand a little wand [1] to indicate the part he mentions, though in many cases the demonstration was made by a second doctor of medicine known as the demonstrator, whilst the lecturer read his remarks. At either end of the table was an assistant—the Masters of the Anatomy—with scalpel in hand ready to expose the different structures, and to clear up any

[1] The College of Physicians still possess a little whalebone rod tipped with silver which Harvey is said to have used in demonstrating his Lumleian lectures.

points of difficulty. The audience grouped themselves in the most advantageous positions for seeing and hearing, though in some cases places were assigned to them according to age and rank.

The lecturer upon Anatomy, apart from the fact that he was a Doctor of Physic was a person of considerable importance in the sixteenth century. The greatest care was taken of him, as may be understood from the directions which the Barber Surgeons gave to their Stewards in Anatomy or those members of the Company who were appointed to supervise the arrangements for the lectures. They were ordered " to see and provide that there be every year a mat about the hearth in the Hall that Mr. Doctor be made not to take cold upon his feet, nor other gentlemen that do come and mark the Anatomy to learn knowledge. And further that there be two fine white rods appointed for the Doctor to touch the body where it shall please him ; and a wax candle to look into the body, and that there be always for the doctor two aprons to be from the shoulder downwards and two pair of sleeves for his whole arm with tapes, for change for the said Doctor, and not to occupy one Apron and one pair of sleeves every day which is unseemly. And the Masters of the Anatomy that be about the body to have like aprons and sleeves every day both white and clean. That if the Masters of the Anatomy that be about the Doctor do not see these things ordered and that their knives, probes, and other instruments be fair and clean accordingly with Aprons and sleeves, if they do lack any of the said things afore rehearsed he shall forfeit for a fine to the Hall forty shillings."

The whole business of a public anatomy was conducted with much ceremony, and every detail was regulated by precedent. The exact routine in the Barber Surgeons' Company is laid down in another series of directions. The clerk or secretary is instructed in his duties in the following words: "So soon as the body is brought in deliver out your tickets which must be first filled up as followeth four sorts :— The first form, to the Surgeons who have served the office of Master you must say : Be pleased to attend &c. with which summons you send another for the Demonstrations : to those below the Chair [*i.e.,* who have not filled the office of Master of the Company] you say : Our Masters desire your Company in your Gown and flat Cap &c. with the like notice for the Demonstrations as you send to the ancient Master Surgeons. To the Barbers, if ancient masters, you

say : Be pleased to attend in your Gown only, and ir
below the Chair, then : Our Masters desire &c. as to
the others above, but without the tickets for the
demonstrations.

"The body being by the Masters of Anatomy
prepared for the lecture (the Beadles having first given
the Doctor notice who is to read) and having taken
orders from the Master or Upper Warden [of the
Company] of the Surgeons' side concerning the same,
you meet the whole Court of Assistance [*i.e.*, the
Council] in the Hall Parlour where every gentlemen
cloathes himself [*i.e.*, puts on his livery or gown], and
then you proceed in form to the Theatre. The
Beadles going first, next the Clerk, then the Doctor,
and after him the several gentlemen of the Court ; and
having come therein, the Doctor and the rest of the
Company being seated, the Clerk walks up to the
Doctor and presents him with a wand and retires
without the body of the Court [*i.e.*, the theatre in
which the assemblage of the company technically
constituted a " court "] until the lecture is over when
he then goes up to the Doctor and takes the wand
from him with directions when to give notice for the
reading in the afternoon which is usually at five
precisely, and at one of the clock at noon, which he

pronounces with a distinct and audible voice by saying, This Lecture, Gentlemen, will be continued at five of the clock precisely. Having so said he walks out before the Doctor, the rest of the Company following down to the Hall parlour where they all dine, the Doctor pulling off his own robes and putting on the Clerk's Gown first, which it has always been usual for him to dine in. And after being plentifully regaled they proceed as before until the end of the third day, which being over (the Clerk having first given notice in the forenoon that the lecture will be continued at five of the clock precisely (at which time the same will be ended) he attends the Doctor in the clothing room where he presents him folded up in a piece of paper the sum of ten pounds, and where afterwards he waits upon the Masters of Anatomy and presents each of them in like manner with the sum of three pounds, which concludes the duty of the Clerk on this account.

" N.B.—The Demonstrator, by order of the Court of Assistants, is allowed to read to his pupils after the public lecture is over for three days and till six of the clock on each day and no longer, after which the remains of the body is decently interred at the expence of the Masters of Anatomy, which usually amounts unto the sum of three pounds seven shillings and fivepence."

The study of Anatomy seems to have been regarded universally as an exhausting occupation, for throughout Europe it was the custom to present the auditors with wine and spices after each lecture, unless some more substantial refreshment was provided.

Harvey's lectures at the College of Physicians were probably given with similar ceremony to those just described. His first course was delivered on Tuesday, Wednesday, and Thursday, April 16, 17, and 18, 1616. On the following Tuesday, April 23rd, Shakespeare died at Stratford-on-Avon, and on the succeeding Thursday, April 25th, he was buried in the chancel of the parish church.

At the beginning of his lectures Harvey lays down the following excellent canons for his guidance, of which the sixth seems to indicate that he was acquainted with the works of John of Arderne—

1. To show as much as may be at a glance, the whole belly for instance, and afterwards to subdivide the parts according to their position and relations.

2. To point out what is peculiar to the actual body which is being dissected.

3. To supply only by speech what cannot be shown on your own credit and by authority.

4. To cut up as much as may be in the sight of the audience.

5. To enforce the right opinion by remarks drawn from far and near, and to illustrate man by the structure of animals according to the Socratic rule [given by Aristotle and affixed as an extract to the title-page of the lectures [1]]. To bring in points beyond mere anatomy in relation to the causes of diseases, and the general study of nature with the object of correcting mistakes and of elucidating the use and actions of parts for the use of anatomy to the physician is to explain what should be done in disease.

6. Not to praise or dispraise other anatomists, for all did well, and there was some excuse even for those who are in error.

7. Not to dispute with others, or attempt to confute them, except by the most obvious retort, for three days is all too short a time [to complete the work in hand].

8. To state things briefly and plainly, yet not letting anything pass unmentioned which can be seen.

[1] P. 54.

9. Not to speak of anything which can be as well explained without the body or can be read at home.

10. Not to enter into too much detail, or into too minute a dissection, for the time does not permit.

11. To serve in their three courses according to the glass (*i.e.*, to allot a definite time to each part of the body). In the first day's lectures the abdomen, nasty, yet recompensed by its infinite variety. In the second day's lecture the parlour [*i.e.*, the thorax ?]. In the third day's lecture the divine banquet of the brain.

Harvey adheres pretty closely in his visceral lecture to the programme which he had thus laid down for his own guidance.

The first set of notes deal with the outside of the body, and the abdomen and its contents. The second portion contains an account of the chest and its contents ; whilst the third portion is devoted to a consideration of the head with the brain and its nerves. Only nine pages of the ninety-eight which the book contains are allotted to the heart. The scheme of the lectures is first to give a general introduction in which the subject is arranged under different headings, and then to consider each part under a variety of subheadings. Harvey's playfulness is shown even in the introduction. Each main division is indicated by a roughly drawn hand, and each hand is made to point with a different finger. The first hand points with its little finger, and has the other fingers bent, though the thumb is outstretched as if applied to the nose of the lecturer. The next heading is indicated by an extended ring finger, the next by the middle finger, whilst the later ones are mere " bunches of fives," or single amputated digits. In his description of the abdomen Harvey shows himself fully alive to the evils of tight-lacing, for, in speaking of the causes of difficult respiration he says, " young girls by lacing : unde cut their laces." After a full discussion of the situation and functions of the various parts of the abdominal viscera, he passes on to the thorax and enunciates his memorable discovery in these remarkable words, which are initialled to show that he thought the idea was peculiarly his own :—

" It is plain from the structure of the heart that the blood is passed continuously through the lungs to the aorta as by the two clacks of a water bellows to raise water.

" It is shown by the application of a ligature that the passage of the blood is from the arteries into the veins.

" Whence it follows that the movement of the blood is constantly in a circle, and is brought about by the beat of the heart. It is a question therefore whether this is for the sake of nourishment or rather for the preservation of the blood and the limbs by the communication of heat, the blood cooled by warming the limbs being in turn warmed by the heart."

Here the notes on the heart end abruptly, and Harvey passes on to consider the lungs. These few sentences show, however, that he had discovered the circulation, and that although he delayed for twelve years to make his results public he was unable to add any important fact in the interval.

The College of Physicians still preserve some interesting memorials of this portion of Harvey's Lumleian lectures. They consist of a series of six dissections of the blood vessels and nerves of the human body, which are traditionally reported to have been made by Harvey himself. The dissections are displayed upon six boards of the size of the human body, and they exhibit the complete system of the blood vessels separated from the other parts so as to form diagrams of the circulatory apparatus. They have been made with such care that one of the series still shows the semilunar valves at the beginning of the aorta. These "tabulae Harveianae" were kept for many years at Burley-on-the-Hill, the seat of the Earls of Winchelsea, one of whose ancestors—Heneage Finch—the Lord Chancellor Nottingham, married Elizabeth, a daughter of William Harvey's younger brother Daniel.

Harvey continued his Lumleian lectures year by year, but we know nothing more of them until 1627, when he delivered a series of lectures upon the anatomy and physiology of the human body, more especially of the arm and leg, with a description of the veins, arteries, and nerves of these parts. This was clearly the Muscular lecture, and if he had followed the course prescribed by the founders of the lecture it should have been given in the years 1619 and 1625, for the years 1621 and 1627 should not have embraced an anatomical course. The notes of the Muscular lecture are in the Sloane collection at the British Museum, where they have been preserved by as happy an accident as those of the much more important Visceral lecture. The volume consists of 121 leaves with writing upon both sides of each page. The notes are as rough and as concise as those of the Visceral lecture, and the language is again a mixture of Latin and homely English. They show, like the treatise on development, that Harvey had by no means emancipated himself from the trammels of authority. He felt for Aristotle what many of us still feel for John Hunter, for he said of his great Master that he had hardly ever made any discovery in connection with the structure of an animal but that Aristotle either knew of it or explained it. He seems to have given his fertile imagination full play in these lectures, and amongst a wealth of similes we find :—

An cerebrum rex [Whether the Brain is to be looked upon as King,]

Nervi Magistratus [The nerves as his ministers,]

Ramuli nervorum officiales [and the branches of the nerves as their subordinates,]

Musculi Cives, populus [whilst the muscles are the burgesses or the commonalty].

And in another place :—

An Cerebrum, Master : Spina his mate.

Nervi, Boteswayne.

Musculi, Saylors.

"There are similar comparisons," says Sir George

Paget, who analysed these lectures, and published an account of the manuscript, "of the brain with a military commander, the leader of an orchestra, an architect, and the prius motor, and of the nerves and muscles with the respective subordinate officers."

His treatise on the movement of the blood must have been passing through the press at the time he gave these lectures, and the subject of the circulation must therefore have been uppermost in his mind. He compares the heart to the other organs thus :—

An WH. potius.

Cor, imperator, Rex. [Whether the heart should not rather be considered as the Emperor or King,]

Cerebrum, Judex, Serjeant-Major, praepositi [whilst the brain is the judge, serjeant-major, or monitor].

THE ZENITH

YEAR by year Harvey continued to deliver the Lumleian lectures at the College of Physicians and to attend his patients at St. Bartholomew's Hospital. He soon obtained an important and fairly lucrative practice. On the 3rd of February, 1618, he was appointed Physician Extraordinary to James I. or in the language of the time, "The king, as a mark of his singular favour, granted him leave to consult with his ordinary physicians as to his Majesty's health," and at the same time he promised him the post of a Physician in Ordinary as soon as one should become vacant. This promise he was unable to fulfil, but it was redeemed by his son Charles I., who appointed Harvey a Physician in Ordinary in 1631 and remained his friend through life.

We can still obtain glimpses of Harvey's practice

during the ten years which preceded the issue in 1628 of his "Anatomical Essay on the Movement of the Heart and Blood." Aubrey tells us that "he rode on horseback with a footcloth to visit his patients, his man still following on foot, as the fashion then was, which was very decent, now quite discontinued. The judges rode also with their footclothes to Westminster Hall, which ended at the death of Sir Robert Hyde, Lord Chief Justice. Anthony, Earl of Shaftesbury, would have revived it, but several of the judges being old and ill-horsemen would not agree to it." The footcloth was originally a mark of dignity, and it is still seen in its full splendour hanging over the backs of the horses in a state pageant and in a debased form on those drawing the hearse at a funeral.

Besides being physician to the household of the king, Harvey seems to have held a similar position in the households of the most distinguished nobles and men of eminence. He treated amongst others the Lord Chancellor Bacon, always a weak and ailing man, and somewhat of a hypochondriac. Bacon, with the curious lack of individuality which has so often obscured the greatness of the highest form of speculative genius, entirely failed to impress the more practical mind of Harvey, who would not allow him to be a great philosopher, though he esteemed him much for his wit and style. Speaking of him in derision, he told Aubrey, "He writes philosophy like a Lord Chancellor." Nothing, perhaps, brings home to us more clearly the real greatness of Aristotle and the immeasurably superior position to which he attained than this want of sympathy between Harvey and Bacon. Both were master minds, both were working on the lines laid down by Aristotle himself, yet their results were so little in accord that whilst Bacon, working upon the theoretical side, succeeded in undermining his authority, Harvey taking the experimental side actually enhanced his lustre.

The following notice of Harvey's practice is preserved in the Domestic Series of the State Papers. It is dated the 18th of November, 1624, and it is interesting, because it shows that the country gentry had to obtain special leave if they wanted to stay in London during the winter :—

" Mr. ATTORNEY.

" His Majesty is graciously pleased in regard of the indisposition of health of Sir William Sandis and his Lady and the great danger of their remove into the Country, as appears by the enclosed certificate of Dr.

Harvey, to dispense with their stay in London this winter season, notwithstanding the proclamation. And accordingly requires you to take present order for their indemnity that no charge or trouble come upon them for their stay in London this winter for which they have his Majesty's leave."

But the patient did not improve under Harvey's care, though he kept him alive, for it is noted again on the 1st of January, 1627–8 :—

"I do hereby certify of a truth that Sir William Sands is in body infirm and subject to those diseases (which) in the country he cannot receive remedy for, nor undergo and perform that course of physic which is fitting for his recovery.

"WILLIAM HARVEY."

The Domestic Series of State Papers also contains a letter showing that Harvey was attending the Lord Treasurer for a fit of the stone on the 23rd of May, 1627.

The year 1628 may fairly be looked upon as the crowning year of Harvey's scientific life. It was that in which he published at Frankfort-on-the-Main his matured account of the circulation of the blood. After its publication he was sometimes heard to say that "he fell mightily in his practice," for it was believed by the vulgar that he was crack-brained, and all the physicians were against him. Such ideas probably occurred to him in his later years when he was depressed by repeated attacks of gout. But party feeling ran high, and was even greater than professional jealousy at a time when Harvey was very closely connected with the losing side. Some of his contemporaries took advantage of the double meaning attaching to the word Circulator which Celsus applies to a merry andrew. It was also said about him that "though all of his profession would allow him to be an excellent anatomist, I never heard of many that admired his therapeutic way. I knew several practitioners in this town that would not have given threepence for one of his bills, as a man can hardly tell by his bills what he did aim at." The apothecaries at this time were accustomed to buy up the bills or prescriptions of the leading physicians in much the same manner and for the same purpose that a clinical clerk or a dresser in a hospital now treasures up the prescriptions of his physician or surgeon. We can afford to smile at these pieces of contemporary criticism by empirics, for we remember that as the apothecaries objected to the practice of Harvey, the attorneys led by Coke sneered at the legal knowledge of Bacon, but in neither case has the verdict of posterity ratified that of contemporary opinion.

Harvey early attained to high office in the College of Physicians, then but a small body, though it contained as it has always done, the picked men of the medical profession. Here he was elected a Censor in 1613, an office to which he was reappointed in 1625 and again in 1629. The Censors were four fellows of the College appointed annually, with power "to supervise, watch, correct, and govern" those who practised physic in London or within the statutory limit of seven miles, whether members of the College or not. They had power to punish by fine and summary imprisonment in the Wood Street Counter, and the name of Harvey occurs more than once about this time in connection with proceedings taken by the College against quacks or "Empirics" as they were then called.

The Censors attended by the representatives of the Society of Apothecaries were empowered to visit the shops of the apothecaries in London to "search, survey, and prove whether the medicines, wares, drugs, or any thing or things, whatsoever in such shop or shops contained and belonging to the art and mystery of an apothecary be wholesome, meet and fit for the cure, health, and ease of his Majesty's subjects." These inquisitorial visits were made at irregular times every summer and autumn. The procession, consisting of the Censors with the Wardens and the Beadle of the Society of Apothecaries, started at one o'clock, and before six in the afternoon from twenty to thirty shops had been visited. At each shop the visitors entered and asked for a few drugs selected at random. They then examined the stock from which the supply was taken, as well as the individual sample offered, a few rough tests were applied, and if the drugs were found to be bad or adulterated they were at once destroyed by the simple but effectual method of throwing them out into the street. The records of each visitation were kept in a book belonging to the College of Physicians.

Dr. Robert Pitt, Censor in 1687 and again in 1702 has left us an interesting account of the results of such a visitation, which in all probability did not differ materially from those which it was Harvey's duty to conduct. The Transcript of the Deposition in the time of Dr. Pitt's censorship runs thus—

Mr. G——'s Shop.

London Laudanum without either colour or smell.

Oxycroceum without saffron.

Pil. Ruff. no colour of saffron. [This was a pill largely used as a preservative against the plague. It contained myrrh, aloes, and saffron.]

Mr. R——'s Shop.

Diascordium dark and thin, without a due proportion of the gums. [It was a compound electuary containing no less than 19 ingredients. It was considered useful in the treatment of epilepsy, megrim, want of appetite, wind, colic, and malignant fevers.]

London Laudanum, a dry, hard substance, without smell or colour.

Mr. S——'s Shop.

Diascordium too thin (let down with honey, I suppose).

Venice treacle, a thin body, much candied. [This, like Diascordium and Mithridate, was one of the complex electuary medicines of the Middle Ages. Its proportions were almost word for word those recommended by Galen in his treatise, Περὶ 'Αντιδότων. It was also known as the treacle of Andromachus.]

London Laudanum, a dry, hard substance, without smell or colour.

Mr. G——'s Shop.

Diascordium thin bodied, much candied.

Venice treacle thin, candied, without its proportions.

London Laudanum, a dry, hard substance.

Mr. G.——'s Shop.

Paracelsus without its powders or gums.

Oxycroceum of a dark colour.

Diascordium of a thin substance.

Gascoin's powder without bezoar. [This was the compound powder of crabs' claws much used in measles, smallpox, and all spotted fevers. It contained in addition to bezoar and crabs' eyes, red coral, white amber, hart's horn philosophically prepared, and jelly of English vipers' skins.]

London Laudanum hard, without smell or colour.

Pil. ex duobus without the oil of cloves. [This was reckoned one of the best and most general pills in the Dispensatory, being strong but yet safe. It was especially useful against scurvy, dropsy, and gout. It consisted of colocynth, scammony, and cloves.]

Mr. S——'s Shop.

Diascordium of a thin body without the gums.

Mithridate no colour of saffron. [This was the remedy *par excellence* until the middle of the eighteenth century. It was said to owe its name to Mithridates, King of Pontus and Bithynia, who invented it. Like Diascordium it was an electuary, though it was more complex, for it contained over fifty ingredients. Mithridate was reputed to cure the bites and stings of any poisonous animal. It expelled poison and cured nearly every disease. It was not only a cure, but a preservative against the plague and all pestilential and infectious fevers.]

London Laudanum neither smell nor colour.

Liquid Laudanum no smell, thin, no colour of saffron.

Gascoin's powder without bezoar.

A part of Harvey's time was employed in duties of

this nature, but on the 3rd of December, 1627, he was appointed to the still more important office of " Elect." The " Elects " were eight in number. They were chosen from the most cunning and expert men of the faculty in London. It was their duty once in a year to select one of their number to fill the office of President, whilst as a Board with a quorum of three they formed the examiners of those who desired to exercise or practise physic throughout England, whose fitness they certified by letters testimonial. These examinations were conducted at the house of the President, where, on the 9th of December, 1629, Harvey examined and approved that Dr. James Primrose who soon became the most malignant opponent of his teaching. Primrose was a pupil of Riolanus, Professor of Anatomy in Paris, and was well described as the quibbling advocate of exploded teaching.

Harvey seems to have comported himself well even in the high position of an elect, for in 1628 he was made Treasurer of the College, an office to which he was re-elected in 1629, so that he must have shown some of the business capacity which was so marked a feature in the other members of his family.

In this year Harvey received the commands of the

King to accompany the Duke of Lennox (born in 1612) who was sent to travel abroad. This was the first interval in the monotony of his professional life since Harvey's return to England from Padua. But the times soon became so broken that he never afterwards settled down again into anything like his old habits. He was nearly fifty-two years of age when, in September, 1629, the Lord Secretary Dorchester procured a licence for James Stuart, Duke of Lennox, to travel for three years taking with him Dr. Topham, Dean of Lincoln, John St. Almain, and eight other servants. The Duke, who was advanced to the Dukedom of Richmond by letters patent dated the 8th of August, 1641, afterwards became Lord Great Chamberlain, and held many honourable appointments in the reign of Charles I. Clarendon often mentions him as a young nobleman of the highest principles, and his staunch loyalty to the King is shown by his being one of the four Lords who with Juxon attended their master's funeral at Windsor. He subscribed no less than £40,000 towards the expenses of the war.

Harvey had to make many arrangements before he could leave England. On the 3rd of December, 1629, he collected the seven "Elects" at his house, and, after a sumptuous banquet, he asked their permission to resign his office of Treasurer at the College of Physicians, a request which was immediately granted. On the 21st of January he applied for leave of absence from his post of physician to St. Bartholomew's Hospital, for the Minutes record—

"Curia tent. Sabti xxi die Januarii 1629–30.
"In presence of Sir Robt. Ducy Knight & Barronet, President (and others).

"DR. HARVEY.

"This day Dr. Harvey Physician to this hospital declares to this court that he is commanded by the Kings most excellent majesty to attend the illustrious Prince the now Duke of Lenox in his travels beyond the seas and therefore desireth this court would allow of [Edmund] Smith, Doctor in Physic for his deputy in performance of the office of physician for the poor of this hospital during his absence. It is thought fit that the Governors of this Hospital shall have further knowledge & satisfaction of the sufficiency of the said Mr. Smith. Then they to make their choice either of him or of some other whom they shall think meet for the execution of the same place during the absence of the said Dr. Harvey."

Leave of absence having been thus granted by the College of Physicians and St. Bartholomew's Hospital, Harvey had only to get a substitute for his Court appointment. An undated letter written from abroad by Harvey to Mr. Secretary Dorchester, says : "Before I went I entreated and appointed Dr. Chambers and Dr. Bethune [physicians in ordinary to the King] and one Dr. Smith of London, one of them at all occasions to perform the duty for me ; and I acquainted the household therewith [though] it is not usual [to do so] for serjeant [surgeon] Primrose was away above a year (and he is surgeon of the household) and yet none were put in his place to wait whilst he was in Germany with my Lord Marquis. Sir Theodore Mayerne [too] in Switzerland in King James his time was away very long and none put in his place." The letter was written upon an unfounded report which had reached Harvey in his absence that Dr. Adam Moesler " hath gotten to be appointed to wait in my place for the household."

Dr. Aveling's care has traced the course of the travellers on this journey. Sir Henry Mervyn writes to Nicholas (clerk of the Council) under the date of the 28th of July, 1630, "of having put over my Lord Duke [Lennox] for the coast of France." The journey was therefore begun at this date, but the Duke and his retinue seem to have stayed for a time in the towns upon the French coast, for on the 2nd of August Sir Henry Mervyn writes that he is going to attend the Duke of Lennox, and purposes to be in the Downs, &c. ; and again on the 10th of August he says he has landed the Duke of Lennox at Dieppe. On the 23rd of September of the same year Edward Dacres writes to Secretary Dorchester that the Duke of Lennox is now settled in Paris for the winter ; and again on the 22nd of November, saying that the Duke is willing to stay in Paris, and that " in the spring he intends the tour de France, and in the end of the summer to go into Italy, unless the continuance of the wars or the plague hinder him."

Dacres writes again, on the 5th of April, 1631, that the Duke is still in Paris but he thinks of going out of town for a few days. Harvey, however, was in London on the 8th of October and on the 22nd of December, 1630, so that he probably joined the Duke in Paris in the spring or early summer of 1631. Nothing is known of the movements of the party after April, until Dacres writes again to Dorchester in August, 1631, saying : " Blois proved a place not long to be endured by my Lord because of the plague which grew hot there, as Tours likewise, where we made little stay, so that we came down to Saumurs there to pass the dog days from whence we are now parting they being at an end. My Lord hath continually been in good health and intends now to follow your Lordship's directions this winter for Spain whither we are now bending our course (*viâ* Bordeaux) where we shall be before the latter end of September."

It is probably of this part of his journey that Harvey writes to Viscount Dorchester, "the miseries of the countries we have passed and the hopes of our good success and such news your Honour hath from better hands. I can only complain that by the way we could scarce see a dog, crow, kite, raven or any other bird, or any thing to anatomise, only some few miserable people, the relics of the war and the plague where famine had made anatomies before I came. It is scarce credible in so rich, populous, and plentiful countries as these were that so much misery and desolation, poverty and famine should in so short a time be, as we have seen. I interprete it well that it will be a great motive for all here to have and procure assurance of settled peace. It is time to leave fighting when there is nothing to eat, nothing to be kept, and nothing to be gotten." The forecast was correct. The Mantuan war was soon afterwards brought to a close by the mediation of Pope Urban VIII. It was one of the minor struggles in which Richelieu's attempts to consolidate the power of his master were counteracted by the combined efforts of Spain and the Empire, for in the end Charles of Nevers was left to enjoy his Duchy of Mantua. The plague, too, was especially virulent in Northern Italy about this time. It was reckoned that above a million died of it in the territories which Lennox and his retinue would have traversed to reach Venice; and 33,000 are said to have died in Verona alone. It was partly for this reason and partly, perhaps, from political motives, that the travellers turned off into Spain instead of visiting Italy, as had been intended. In February, 1632, Sir Thomas Edmonde, writing to Sir Harry Vane, says: "the Duke of Lenox has been made a Grand in Spain;" and it was about this time that the party returned homewards.

Harvey was certainly in England on the 26th of March, 1632, for on that day he drew up a set of rules for the Library of the College of Physicians, towards a site for which he had subscribed £100 on the 22nd of December, 1630. The necessity for a new set of rules to govern the use of the Library seems to have been due to an important bequest of 680 volumes presented by Dr. Holsbosch, a graduate in medicine, and a German who had practised surgery and physic in England for fifty years, though he had not attached himself to the College. The new regulations laid down that the key of the room was to remain in the keeping of the President, whilst the key of the book-cases was kept by the Senior Censor. The Library was to be open on all College days to the Fellows, Candidates, and Licentiates; but no book was to be taken away from the College without leave from the President and Censor and the deposit of a "sufficient caution" for its value. Harvey was also present at a meeting of the College of Physicians on the last day of May, 1632, when he signed a petition to the King, praying him to limit the sale of certain poisons unless the purchaser was willing to give his name.

There is no record of the exact date at which Harvey was made Physician in Ordinary to the King Charles I., though the time is fixed approximately by the following extract from the minutes at St. Bartholomew's Hospital :—

" Monday 25 April 1631 at a Court [of Governors]

held in the Mansion house in the presence of Sir Robert Ducy Lord Mayor, President.

"DR. ANDREWES

"It is granted that Richard Andrewes Doctor of Physic shall. have the reversion, next avoidance and place of physician to this hospital after the death, resignation or other departure of Doctor Harvey now physician to this hospital late sworn Physician in Ordinary for his Majesty's Household, with the yearly stipend thereunto now belonging."

The actual date of his appointment seems to have been at some time during the quarter ending Lady Day, 1630, for the Calendar of State Papers (Domestic Series) contains the record, "3 July 1635. To William Harvey, one of his Majesty's physicians in ordinary, his annuity for a year ending at Our Lady Day 1631 £300." And again on the 17th of July, 1635, "Dr. William Harvey £25;" and a few months later, on the 5th of February, 1635–6—"Dr. William Harvey upon his annuity of £300 per annum £150." These entries also make it appear that although his salary amounted to the considerable sum of £300 a year, it was paid very irregularly and by small instalments.

Harvey's appointment as personal physician to the King seems to have brought him into close connection with his master, and it was no doubt at this time that Charles allowed him to obtain the intimate knowledge of the habits and structure of the deer which was afterwards turned to such good use in the treatise on Development. Harvey, in fact, became the personal friend of his king, he accompanied him everywhere, and consequently took a share in the hunting excursions to which his Majesty was so devoted.

This constant attendance at Court naturally interfered with Harvey's professional duties, and his colleagues at St. Bartholomew's Hospital soon began to complain of his absence.

" At a Court held on Sunday 19 January 1632–3,
" In presence of Sir Robert Ducie Knight &
Baronet, President.

" DR. HARVY

" It hath been thought convenient upon complaint of some of the chirurgions of this hospital that whereas Doctor Harvy physician for the poor of the said hospital by reason of his attendance on the King's Majesty cannot so constantly be present with the

poor as heretofore he hath been, but sometimes
doth appoint his deputy for the same. That there-
for Doctor Andrewes physician in reversion of the
same place to this hospital in the absence of Doctor
Harvey do supply the same place whereby the said
poor may be more respected and Doctor Andrewes
the better acquainted to perform the same office
when it shall fall [vacant], and in the mean time to
be recompensed by this court yearly as shall be
thought fit. This order not to prejudice Dr. Harvy
in his yearly fee or in any other respect than
aforesaid."

Early in 1633 Harvey received the commands of
Charles I. to attend him on his journey to Scotland, and the annexed Minute shows that he again
endeavoured to gain the permission of the Governors
of the hospital to allow Dr. Smith to act for him
in his absence.

"13 May Anno Domini 1633.

"This day came into this Compting house Doctor
Smith physician by the appointment of Dr. Harvey,
physician to this hospital who is to attend the
King's Majesty into Scotland and tendered his

service to Mr. Treasurer and other the Governors for the poor in the behalf and absence of Doctor Harvey. Answer was made by Mr. Treasurer that Doctor Andrewes physician in reversion to this house was by the Court ordered to attend the occasions of this house in the absence of Doctor Harvey and to have allowance from this house accordingly. Nevertheless if Doctor Smith pleased to accompany Doctor Andrewes in the business, this house would be very well content, unto which Doctor Smith replied that if Dr. Andrewes was appointed and did perform accordingly, there is no need of two."

It seems to be evident from these Minutes that Dr. Smith was Harvey's nominee. He was his life-long friend, and he only survived a fortnight the opening of the Harveian Museum, of which he was the most active promoter. Dr. Andrewes, on the other hand, had powerful City influence to back him. He was a distinguished graduate of St. John's College, Oxford. He had been educated at the Merchant Taylors' School, and stood high in the favour of the Merchant Taylors' Company. He died the 25th of July, 1634.

Charles' tour in. Scotland was fraught with the most momentous consequences both to himself and his kingdom. He was crowned with great pomp in the Abbey Church at Holyrood, and the rochet worn by the Bishop of Moray when he preached before the assembled Court on this occasion was an innovation which gave the greatest offence to the people. Their discontent was still further increased by an order from the King enjoining the ministers to wear surplices and the Bishops vestments instead of the Geneva gown to which they had been accustomed since the Reformation. The dissatisfaction thus aroused culminated in the Liturgy tumults of 1637, when Jenny Deans launched her stool at the head of the Bishop of St. Giles whilst he was preaching in Edinburgh. The tumults in turn led to the formation of " the Tables " and to the taking of " the Covenant," which are so familiar to every student of the history of the Civil War.

Harvey must have been in close attendance upon the King during the whole of his stay in Scotland, but he probably interested himself very little in the proceedings of the Court or in the hot discussions between the rival sects around him. We know, indeed, that, he was thinking about the method by which a chick is formed within the egg, and that to solve the point he paid a visit to the Bass Rock, of which he gives the following description in the eleventh essay of his treatise on Development :—

" In the barren island of the East Coast of Scotland, such flights of almost every kind of seabirds congregate, that were I to state what I have heard from those who were worthy of credit, I fear I should be held guilty of telling greater stories than they who have committed themselves about the Scottish geese produced as they say from the fruits of certain trees (which they had never seen) that had fallen into the sea.[1] What I have seen myself, however, I will relate truthfully.

[1] The reference is to the passage in Gerarde's " Herbal," giving an account of the miraculous origin of the Solan Goose. It runs : " But what our eyes have seen and hands have touched we shall declare. There is a small island in Lancashire called the Pile of Foulders, wherein are found the broken pieces of old and bruised ships, some whereof have been cast thither by shipwreck, and also the trunks and bodies with the branches of old and rotten trees cast up there likewise, whereon is found a certain spume or froth that in time breedeth unto certain shells, in shape like those of a mussel, but sharper pointed, and of a whitish colour wherein is contained in form like a lace of silk finely woven as it were together, of a whitish colour, one end whereof is fastened unto the inside of the shell, even as the fish of oysters and mussels are ; the other end is made fast to the belly of a rude mass or lump, which in time cometh to the shape and form of a Bird ; when it is perfectly formed the shell gapeth open, and the first thing that appeareth is the aforesaid lace or string ; next come the legs of the bird hanging out, and as it groweth greater it openeth the shell by degrees till at length it is all come forth and hangeth only by

"There is a small island, Scotsmen call it the Bass
(let it serve as a type of all the rest), lying near the
shore, but in deep water. It is so rugged and pre-
cipitous that it might rather be called a huge stone
or rock than an island, for it is not more than a mile
in circumference. The whole surface of the island in
the months of May and June is almost completely
carpeted with nests, birds, and fledglings. There are
so many that you can scarcely avoid stepping upon
them, and when they fly the crowd is so great that it
hides the sun and the sky like a cloud. The scream-
ing and the din too are so great that you can hardly
hear any one speaking close to you. If you look

the bill ; in short space after it cometh to full maturity and falleth into
the sea, where it gathereth feathers and groweth to a fowl bigger than a
mallard and lesser than a goose, having black legs and bill or beak, and
feathers black and white, spotted in such manner as is our Magpie . . .
which the people of Lancashire call by no other name than a tree goose ;
which place aforesaid and all those parts adjoining do so much abound
therewith, that one of the best is bought for threepence. For the truth
hereof if any doubt, may it please them to repair unto me, and I shall
satisfy them by the testimony of good witnesses " (Gerarde's " Herbal,"
A.D. 1636, p. 1588, chap. 171. " Of the Goose Tree, Barnacle Tree, or
the Tree-bearing Goose ").

A solan goose was looked upon for many years as a delicacy. Pennant
states that about the middle of the seventeenth century a young one was
sold for 20d. He also quotes the following newspaper cutting :—
" SOLAN GOOSE.—There is to be sold by John Walton, Jun., at his stand
at the Poultry, Edinburgh, all lawful days in the week, wind and weather
serving, good and fresh solan geese. Any who have occasion for the
same, may have them at reasonable rates.—Aug. 5, 1768."

down upon the sea, as if from a tower or tall precipice, whichever way you turn you will see an enormous number of different kinds of birds skimming about and gaping for their prey, so that the sea looks like a pond which is swarming with frogs in springtime, or like those sunny hills looked at from below when they are covered with numerous flocks of sheep and goats. If you sail round the island and look up you see on every ledge, shelf, and recess innumerable flocks of birds of every sort and size, more numerous than the stars seen at night in the unclouded moonless sky, and if you watch the flights that come and go incessantly, you might imagine that it was a mighty swarm of bees. I should hardly be believed if I said what a large revenue was obtained annually from the feathers and from the old nests (used for firing) and from the eggs, which are boiled and then sold, though the owner told me himself. There is one feature, too, which seems to be especially worthy of note because it bears closely upon my argument and is clear proof of what I have just said about the crowd of birds. The whole island shines brilliantly white to those who approach it, and the cliffs are as bright as if they were made of the whitest chalk ; yet the natural colour of the rock is dusky and black. It is due to a brittle crust of the whitest colour that is spread over all and gives the island its whiteness and brilliancy, a crust of the same consistence, colour, and nature as the shell of an egg."

Harvey was in London again on the 5th of October, 1633, for on this day, at St. Bartholomew's Hospital, " upon the motion of Dr. Harvey, physician to this house, it is thought fit that Tuesday se'night in the afternoon be the time that the Governors shall hear himself and the Chirurgeons upon some particulars concerning the good of the poor of this house and reformation of some orders conceived to be in this house. And the Chirurgeons and the Apothecary to be warned to meet accordingly. And Mr. Alderman Mowlson, Sir Maurice Abbott, Mr. Alderman Perry, and others the Governors here present, are intreated to meet at the Compting house to hear and determine the same." Accordingly, on the 15th of October some radical changes were made in the management of the hospital, as is indicated in the next Minute. The articles are introduced with the following preface, which gives a clear account of the high estimation in which Harvey's services were held at this time. " This day Dr. Harvey, physician to this hospital, presented to this court [of Governors] certain articles for the good and benefit of the poor of this house, which the Governors have taken into their considerations and do allow and order them to be put in practice. And all defaults in the not performance of any of the said articles to be corrected and amended by the Governors as they in their discretions shall think fit and convenient.

"Forasmuch as the poor of this house are increased to a greater number than formerly have been, to the great charge of this hospital, and to the greater labour and more necessary attendance of a physician. And being much more also than [it] is conceived one physician may conveniently perform.

"And forasmuch as Dr. Harvey, the now physician to this hospital, is also chosen to be physician to his Majesty, and [is] thereby tied to daily service and attendance on his Majesty,

"It hath been thought fit and so ordered, that there shall be for this present occasion two physicians for this hospital. And that Dr. Andrewes, physician in reversion, be now admitted to be also an immediate physician to this hospital. And to have the salary or yearly fee of £33 6s. 8d. for his pains henceforth during the pleasure of this court.

"And this court, for the long service of the said Dr.

97   H

Harvey to this hospital, and in consideration that he is physician to his Majesty, do give and allow him leave and liberty to dispose of himself and time, and to visit the poor no oftener than he in his discretion shall think fit.

"And it is ordered that Mr. Treasurer shall also pay unto the said Dr. Andrewes the sum of £20 for his pains taken in visiting and prescribing for the poor of this house for this year last past by the direction and at the request of the Governors of this house.

"Also at the suit of the apothecary (for the considerations abovesaid), it is thought fit and so granted, that £10 be yearly added to his salary from Michaelmas last past for and towards the maintenance of a journeyman to be daily present in the apothecary's shop in this hospital to help him in the dispatch of his business during the pleasure of this court.

"Likewise at the motion of Dr. Harvey, it is granted that Mr. Treasurer shall pay unto Dr. Smith, who was the deputy of Dr. Harvey and by him appointed in his absence to visit the poor of this hospital, the sum of £10 in gratuity from this court, and he is thereupon intreated in respect the hospital hath now two physicians, that he do not henceforth trouble himself any more to visit or prescribe to the poor of this hospital."

On the same day (October 15, 1633), " Dr. Harvey, physician to this hospital, presented to this court certain orders or articles by him thought fit to be observed and put in practice, viz. :—

" 1. That none be taken into the Hospital but such as be curable, or but a certain number of such as are incurable.

" Allowed.

" 2. That those that shall be taken in for a certain time be discharged at that time by the Hospitaller, unless they obtain a longer time. And to be discharged at the end of that time also.

" In use.

" 3. That all such are certified by the doctor uncurable, and scandalous or infectious shall be put out of the said house or to be sent to an outhouse,[1] and in case of sudden inconvenience this to be done by the Doctor or Apothecary.

" Allowed.

" 4. That none be taken into any outhouse on the charge of this Hospital but such as are sent from hence.

" Allowed.

---

[1] The outhouses, Sir James Paget tells us, were the Lock Hospitals belonging to St. Bartholomew's Hospital. There were two outhouses, one in Kent Street, Southwark, the other in Kingsland. They were

"5. That no Chirurgion, to save himself labour, take in or present any for the doctor ; otherwise the charge of the Apothecary's shop will be so great, and the success so little, as it will be scandalous to the house.

"Allowed.

"6. That none lurk here for relief only or for slight causes.

"Allowed.

"7. That if any refuse to take their physic, they may be discharged by the Doctor or Apothecary or punished by some order.

"Allowed.

"8. That the Chirurgions, in all difficult cases or where inward physic may be necessary, shall consult with the Doctor, at the times he sitteth once in the week and then the Master [*i.e.*, the Surgeon] himself relate to the Doctor what he conceiveth of the cure and what he hath done therein. And in a decent and

founded originally as Lazar-houses for the use of lepers. The "Lock " in the Borough was used for women ; the "Spital " in Kingsland for men. Each contained about thirty beds and was under the charge of a guider, guide or surgeon, who was appointed by the Governors of the Hospital, and received from them in Harvey's time an annual stipend of four pounds a year and fourpence a day for the diet of each patient under their care.

orderly manner proceed by the Doctor's directions for the good of the poor and credit of the house.[1]

" Agreed unto.

" 9. That no Chirurgion or his man do trepan the head, pierce the body, dismember [amputate], or do any great operation on the body of any but with the approbation and by the direction of the Doctor (when conveniently it may be had) and the Chirurgions shall think it needful to require.

" Agreed unto.

" 10. That no Chirurgion or his man practice by giving inward physic to the poor without the approbation of the Doctor.

" Allowed.

" 11. That no Chirurgion be suffered to perform the cures in this house by his boy or servant without his own oversight or care.

" Allowed.

" 12. That every Chirurgion shall shew and declare unto the Doctor whensoever he shall in the presence

---

[1] This and the two following regulations illustrate in a very remarkable manner the complete subjection in which the physicians held the surgeons in Harvey's time and for many subsequent years. It was not until Abernethy was surgeon to the hospital, at the beginning of the century, that the surgeons were allowed to prescribe more than a black draught or blue pill for their patients until the prescription had been countersigned by one of the physicians.

of the patient require him, what he findeth and what he useth to every external malady ; that so the Doctor being informed may better with judgment order his prescriptions.

"The Chirurgions protest against this.[1]

"13. That every Chirurgion shall follow the direction of the Doctor in outward operations for inward causes for the recovery of every patient under their several cures, and to this end shall once in the week attend the Doctor, at the set hour he sitteth to give directions for the poor.

"Agreed by the Chirurgions.

"14. That the Apothecary, Matron, and Sisters do attend the Doctor when he sitteth to give directions and prescriptions, that they may fully conceive his directions and what is to be done.

"Allowed.

"15. That the Matròn and Sisters shall signify and complain to the Doctor, or Apothecary in the Doctor's absence, if any poor lurk in the house and come not before the Doctor when he sitteth or taketh not his physic but cast it away and abuse it.

"Allowed.

[1] And no wonder, for it meant that their prescriptions were to be made public, whilst those of the Physician were kept secret [sec. 16], and at this time every practitioner had some secret remedy in which he put especial trust.

"16. That the Apothecary keep secret and do not disclose what the Doctor prescribeth nor the prescriptions he useth but to such as in the Doctor's absence may supply his place and that with the Doctor's approbation.

"Allowed."

The ordinances are peremptory, and for many years they governed the action of the Hospital in the control of the patients. Some of them, indeed (as § 6), are still acted upon. They show that Harvey was determined to maintain the superior status of the physicians, and there is but little room to doubt that this was one of the guiding principles of his life. In February, 1620, he was appointed by the College of Physicians to act with Dr. Mayerne and Dr. William Clement in watching the proceedings of the surgeons who were moving Parliament in their own interest. For this purpose he attended a Conference at Gray's Inn on the 17th of February, 1620, and he afterwards went to Cambridge ; but he failed to induce the University to co-operate with the College of Physicians.

On the 4th of July, 1634, Harvey gave a tanned human skin to the College of Physicians, and on the same day by the order of the President he made a speech to the Apothecaries persuading them to conform to the orders of the College.

On the 7th of August, 1634, John Clarke was granted the reversion of Harvey's office of Physician to St. Bartholomew's Hospital "in the room and place of Dr. Andrewes late deceased. And this Hospital do order that after Doctor Harvey his death or departure, there be but one Physician forthwards." Harvey, however, outlived Dr. Clarke, who died in 1653 and was buried in St. Martin's, Ludgate, but as Harvey did not attend the Hospital after 1643 Clarke probably acted as sole Physician to the Hospital for ten years before he died. He was President of the College of Physicians 1645–1649.

The year 1634 was long memorable on account of "the Lancashire witches," whose story is not yet quite forgotten. Their accusation, as in that of the great outbreak at Salem in New England in 1692, began in the lying story of a child. Edward Robinson, a boy of ten, and the son of a woodcutter living on the borders of Pendle Forest in Lancashire, played truant and to excuse himself accused Mother Dickenson of being a witch. The boy, being examined by the magistrates, told his story so openly and honestly that it was at once believed. He said that as he was roaming in one of the glades of the forest picking blackberries he saw two greyhounds which he thought belonged to one of the gentlemen living in the neighbourhood. A hare appearing at the same time he hied on the dogs, but neither of them would stir. Angry at the beasts he took up a switch and was about to punish them when one of the dogs started up as a woman, the other as a little boy. The woman was Mother Dickenson, who offered him money to sell his soul to the devil, but he refused. She then took a bridle out of her pocket, and shaking it over the head of the other little boy he instantly became a horse. Mother Dickenson seized Robinson in her arms and sprang upon the animal. They rode with inconceivable swiftness over forests, fields, bogs, and rivers until they came to a large barn. The witch alighted, and taking him by the hand led him inside. There he saw seven old women pulling at seven halters which hung from the roof. As they pulled, large pieces of meat, lumps of butter, loaves of bread, basins of milk, hot puddings and black puddings fell from the halters on to the floor. Thus a supper was provided, and when it was ready other witches came to share it. Many persons were arrested, for the boy was led about from church to church to identify those he had seen in the barn.

The story made a great sensation and Sir William Pelham wrote to Lord Conway that "the greatest news from the country is of a huge pack of witches which are lately discovered in Lancashire, whereof it is said nineteen are condemned and that there are at least sixty already discovered. It is suspected that they had a hand in raising the great storm wherein his Majesty was in so great danger at sea in Scotland." Popular report exaggerated the number arrested, but seven of the accused were condemned and Bishop Bridgman, of Chester, was requested to examine them. He went to the gaol and found that three had died and another, Janet Hargreaves, lay "past hope of recovery." Of the three examined by him two declared that they had no knowledge of witchcraft, but the third, Margaret Johnson, a widow of sixty, whom the Bishop describes as a person of strong imagination and weak memory, confessed to have been a witch for six years. She told him, "There appeared to her a man in black attire, who said, if she would give him her soul she should have power to hurt whom she would. He called himself Mamilion, and appeared in the shape of a brown-coloured dog, a white cat, and a hare, and in these shapes sucked her blood."

The report of the Bishop to Secretary Coke reached the ears of the King, who commanded Henry Earl of Manchester, the Lord Privy Seal, to write :—

"To Alexander Baker Esq. and Sarjeant Clowes his Majesty's Chirurgions.

"These shall be to will and require you forthwith to make choice of such midwives as you shall think fit to inspect and search the bodies of those women that were lately brought by the sheriff, of the County of Lancaster indicted for witchcraft and to report unto you whether they find about them any such marks as are pretended : wherein the said midwives are to receive instructions from Mr. Dr. Harvey his Majesty's Physician and yourselves.

"Dated at Whitehall the 29 June 1634.

"H. MANCHESTER."

The prisoners, who were then at the Ship Tavern in Greenwich, were brought to London upon the receipt of the King's order. They were examined and the following certificate was issued :—

"Surgeons Hall in Monkwell Street, London.

"2 July A.D. 1634.

"We in humble obedience to your Lordship's command have this day called unto us the Chirurgeons and midwives whose names are hereunder written who have by the directions of Mr. Dr. Harvey (in our presence and his) made diligent search and inspection on those women which were lately brought up from Lancaster and find as followeth, viz. :—

"On the bodies of Jennett Hargreaves, Ffrances Dicconson and Mary Spencer nothing unnatural nor anything like a teat or mark or any sign that any such thing hath ever been.

"On the body of Margaret Johnson we find two things (which) may be called teats. The first in shape like to the teat of a bitch but in our judgement nothing but the skin as it will be drawn out after the application of leeches. The second is like the nipple or teat of a woman's breast, but of the same colour with the rest of the skin without any hollowness or issue for any blood or juice to come from thence."

The report is signed by ten midwives, by Alexander Reid, M.D., the lecturer on Anatomy at the Barber Surgeons' Hall, whom Harvey seems to have deputed to take his place, and by six surgeons evidently chosen from amongst the most eminent of those then practising in London.

The result of this report was that four of the seven convicted witches were pardoned, an exercise of mercy " which may have been due," says Mr. Aveling, " to the enlightened views and prompt and energetic action of Dr. Harvey."

There is no doubt that at this time and throughout his life Harvey practised every branch of his profession. That he was primarily a physician is evident ; that he was a surgeon is shown by the fact that in his will he bequeathed to Dr. Scarborough his "silver instruments of surgery," whilst in his writings he says, " Looking back upon the office of the arteries, I have occasionally, and against all expectation, completely cured enormous sarcoceles by the simple means of dividing or tying the little artery that supplied them, and so preventing all access of nourishment or spirit to the part affected, by which it came to pass that the tumour on the verge of mortification was afterwards easily extirpated with the knife or searing iron."

No one, reading his treatise on Development, can doubt for a moment that he was well versed in the diseases of women and in such practical midwifery as the prejudices and habits of the time allowed him to become familiar. Specialism, indeed, as it is now understood in England, did not exist at this time, though there was a debased form in which men attended only to outward injuries or to internal complaints.

Harvey sometimes got into trouble with his cases, as must always happen even to the most experienced. The records of the Barber Surgeons' Company contain the following notice under the date 17th of November, 1635. It has the marginal note, " Dr. Harvey's ill practise " :—

" This day Wm. Kellett being called here in Court for not making presentation of one of Mr. Kinnersley's maids that died in his charge, he said here in Court that Mr. Doctor Harvey being called to the patient did upon his view of the patient say, that by means of a boulster [poultice ?] the tumour on the temporal muscle could be discussed and his opinion was that there was no fracture but the vomiting came by reason of the foulness of the stomach and to that purpose prescribed physic by

Briscoe the Apothecary, so the patient died by ill practice, the fracture being neglected and the Company not called to the view." When a person was dangerously ill of a surgical disease in London it was long the custom for the practitioner to call in those surgeons who held an official position in the Barber Surgeons' Company. This was called " viewing " the patient. It divided the responsibility whilst it ensured that everything possible was done for the relief of the patient.

In this year too Harvey was ordered by the King to examine the body of Thomas Parr, who is said to have died at the extraordinary age of 152 years and nine months, having survived through the reigns of nine princes. He had lived frugally in Shropshire until shortly before his death, when he was brought to London by Thomas Howard, Earl of Arundel, who showed him to the King. Harvey examined the body on the 16th of November, 1635, the birthday—as he is careful to note—of Her Serene Highness Henrietta Maria, Queen of Great Britain, France, and Ireland. The notes of the autopsy came into the possession of Harvey's nephew Michael, who presented them to Dr. Bett, and they were not printed until 1669, when they were published in Dr. Bett's work "On the Source and Quality of the Blood." The notes give a clear account of the appearances seen upon opening the body, and the very practical conclusion is drawn that as all the internal parts seemed so healthy the old man might have escaped paying the debt due to nature for some little time longer if nothing had happened to interfere with his usual habits. His death is therefore attributed to the change from the pure air of Shropshire to that of London, and to the alteration in his diet which necessarily attended his residence in the house of a great nobleman.

The mutual interest taken by the Earl of Arundel and Harvey in old Parr may have led to the friendship which existed between the two men; perhaps, too, Lord Arundel—the prince of art collectors, to whom we owe the Arundel marbles—had detected in Harvey some similar love of art which rendered him a kindred spirit. It is clear that some bond of union existed, for in the following year—1636— Lord Arundel was sent to Vienna as Ambassador Extraordinary to the Emperor Ferdinand in connection with the peace which the Protestant States of Germany had concluded in 1635. The mission

left England in April, 1636; and the Clarendon
State Papers contain a letter dated from Cologne
in May in which Lord Arundel speaks of a visit
to the Jesuits' new college and church, where he
says "they received me with all civility," and then
adds jokingly, "I found in the College little Doctor
Harvey, who means to convert them." There are
no means of knowing when or why Harvey left
England, but he seems to have attached himself to
the Embassy and to have visited with it the principal
cities on the way to Vienna.

He used the opportunity to make the acquaintance
of the leading scientific men in Germany, as he had
already introduced himself to those in France on a
former journey. On the 20th of May, 1636, he was
at Nuremberg, where he wrote to Caspar Hofmann
offering to demonstrate the circulation of the blood.
He has heard, he says, that Hofmann complained of
his theory, that "he impeached and condemned
Nature of folly and error, and that he had imputed
to her the character of a most clumsy and inefficient
artificer in suffering the blood to become recrudescent,
and making it return again and again to the heart in
order to be reconcocted only to grow effete again in
the arterial system : thus uselessly spoiling the per-

fectly made blood merely to find her something to do." Tradition says that Harvey actually gave this demonstration in public, and that it proved satisfactory to every one except to Hofmann himself. The old man—then past the grand climacteric—remained unconvinced, and as he continued to urge objections Harvey at length threw down his knife and walked out of the theatre.

We are indebted to Aubrey for the following anecdote, which is probably more true than some of his other statements about Harvey, for it is in exact accordance with what we know of his habits. Aubrey says that one of the Ambassador's gentlemen, Mr. William Hollar—the celebrated painter—told him that in this voyage "Dr. Harvey would still be making observations of strange trees and plants, earths, &c., and sometimes [he was] like to be lost. So that my Lord Ambassador would be really angry with him, for there was not only a danger of thieves, but also of wild beasts." How real the danger was may be gauged by remembering that the party was passing through the country devastated by the Thirty Years' War, which had still to drag out its disastrous length until it was brought to a close by the peace of Westphalia in

1648 — a time so productive of lawlessness that it was only two years since Wallenstein, the great Commander-in-chief of the Imperial forces, had been murdered by those who were afterwards publicly rewarded by his Imperial master.

Harvey parted company with the Embassy at Ratisbon, for in a letter dated from there he is spoken of as " Honest little Harvey whom the Earl is sending to Italy about some pictures for his Majesty." From Ratisbon he proceeded to Rome, where the pilgrims' book at the English College shows that he dined in the refectory on the 5th of October, 1636. Dr. Ent dined there the same night. The two travellers probably met by arrangement, for Ent was born at Sandwich, closely allied as a Cinque Port to Folkestone, Harvey's native home. He was educated too in Cambridge — at Sidney Sussex College—and after five years at Padua he took his degree of Doctor of Physic on the 28th of April, 1636. Harvey and Ent had therefore much in common, and they remained firm friends until Harvey died. Ent's love for Harvey led him to defend the doctrine of the circulation against the attacks of Parisanus ; Harvey's love for Ent caused him to entrust to him the essay on Development ;

to be printed or preserved unpublished as Ent should think most fit.

Nothing is known of Harvey's return to England except that he was in London attending to his duties and seeing his patients at the end of the year 1636.

The following certificate appears to be the only record left of his work during the next two years. It is dated the 2nd of December, 1637:

"Having had experience of the disposition and weakness of the body of Sir Thomas Thynne, Knight (who hath been and still is our patient), we testify that we are of opinion that it will be dangerous for the health of his body to travel this winter into the country and place of his usual abode until he hath better recovered his health and strength.

"WILL. HARVEY."

CHAPTER V

THE CIVIL WAR

THE life of Harvey, like that of all his contemporaries, falls naturally into two great divisions. Hitherto it had been passed in peace and learned ease, but for the future much of it was to be spent in camps amongst the alarms of war. War indeed he had seen both in the Mantuan campaign and in the Thirty Years' War in Germany, and the war clouds had been gathering rapidly at home. Few, however, could have imagined that the religious excitement in Scotland, coupled with the results of Strafford's policy in Ireland and the acts of Laud in England, would provoke in a few years an internecine struggle which was not ended even by the execution of him whom in 1640 all looked upon as the Lord's Anointed.

Harvey, perhaps, saw what was coming less clearly

than any of those in a responsible position round the King, and it affected him less. Dr. Bethune, the senior Physician in Ordinary to the King, died in July, 1639, and Harvey was appointed in his place. The post was more valuable than the one he had held, for the College of Physicians contains a memorandum giving an account of the sums of money due to Harvey out of the King's Exchequer. It is docketed—

> " Money due out of the
> Exchequer for my pension
> 21 April 1642
> and also since
> for my pension
> of £400 p. ann."

The appointment carried with it a lodging at Whitehall and certain perquisites which are mentioned in the following order extracted by Mr. Peter Cunningham from the Letter Book of the Lord Steward's office :

" CHARLES R.

" Whereas we have been graciously pleased to admit Doctor Harvey into the place of Physician in Ordinary to our Royal Person, our will and pleasure is that you give order for the settling a diet of three dishes of meat a meal, with all incidents thereunto belonging, upon him the said Doctor Harvey, and the same to begin from the seventeenth day of July last past and to continue during the time that the said Doctor Harvey shall hold and enjoy the said place of Physician in Ordinary to our Royal Persen, for which this shall be your warrant.

"Given at our Court of Whitehall the sixth of December 1639.

"To our trusty and well beloved Councillors Sir Henry Vane and Sir Thomas Jermyn, Knights, Treasurer and Comptroller of our Household or to either of them."

In Scotland the religious riots of 1637 had culminated in the destruction of episcopacy and the formation of the Covenant, acts of rebellion which were assisted by Richelieu in revenge for Charles's opposition to his designs upon Flanders. Preparations were at once made for war. Early in the summer of 1639 the King joined the army under the command of Harvey's friend the Earl of Arundel, and summoned the peers of England to attend him in his progress towards Scotland. His splendid Court, accompanied by nearly 25,000 troops, marched to Berwick. The Scotch forces, with Leslie as their leader, marched South and encamped on Dunse Law, a hill commanding the North Road. The two armies faced each other for a short time, but the King, finding that his troops sided with the Scotch and that defeat was inevitable, concluded a sudden treaty, —signed on the 18th of June, 1639, and known as the " Pacification of Berwick,"—and returned to London. The pacification was not of long duration, but it led to the summoning of that Parliament whose actions soon showed the more sagacious politicians that a civil war was imminent.

The Estates met in Edinburgh on the 2nd of June, 1640, and ordered every one to sign the Covenant under pain of civil penalties. In so doing they acted in direct defiance of the King, and they refused to adjourn at his order. They sent Commissioners to London, but Charles refused to see them, and the Estates then appealed for help to France. A Scotch army was again mustered. It crossed the Tweed and entered England on the 20th of August, 1640. Newcastle, Durham, Tynemouth, and Shields were occupied, whilst the fortresses of Edinburgh and Dumbarton again fell into the hands of the insurgents, who defeated the King's troops at Newburn-on-Tyne.

The King travelled to York, where he held a great Council of Peers on the 24th of September, 1640. By the advice of the Council negotiations were opened with the Scots. Eight Commissioners from their army came to Ripon, and a treaty—called the Treaty of Ripon—was entered upon, though it was not signed until nearly a year later. All that the Scots asked was conceded, and they were promised £300,000 to defray the expenses they had incurred. The armies were then disbanded, and for a time peace seemed to be restored. The King again visited Scotland, and a meeting of the Estates was held, whilst in London the Long Parliament met on the 3rd of November, 1640, and chose Lenthall their Speaker.

Harvey must have witnessed all these events, for he was in close personal attendance upon the King during the whole time. He received a warrant by Royal Sign Manual whilst the King was at York, addressed to the Comptroller of the Household and dated the 25th of September, 1640, by which the King gives £200 to Dr. William Harvey for his diet."

This was in lieu of the three dishes of meat, which in those troublous times were not easily to be obtained.

A month or two later Harvey was in London, for on the 24th of November, 1640, he obtained permission from the College of Physicians to sue the heirs of Baron Lumley in the name of the College to recover the salary of the Lumleian lecturer on surgery and anatomy. Leave was given him, but the political disturbances and Harvey's attendance upon the King appear to have prevented him from carrying out his object. Dr. Munk says that no further mention of this suit occurs in the Annals of the College until the 31st of May, 1647, when "a letter was read from Dr. Harvey desiring the College to grant him a letter of attorney to one Thompson to sue for the anatomical stipend. It was presently generally granted, and shortly afterwards sent him under the general seal." From a manuscript of Dr. Goodall's, in the possession of the College, it appears that Harvey expended at least five hundred pounds in various lawsuits on this subject, which was not settled until some time after his death, and then at the expense of Sir Charles Scarborough, his successor in the chair of the Lumleian Lecturer.

The only notice of Harvey during the year 1641 is

the following entry on page 38 of the Album of
Philip de Glarges, preserved amongst the manuscripts
at the British Museum :

" ' Dii laboribus omnia vendunt.'

" Nobilissimo juveni Medico Phillipo de Glarges
amicitiae ergo libenter scripsit

GUL HARVEUS.

Anglus Med. Reg. et Anatomie professor. Londin :
May 8 A.D. 1641."

["'For toil the Gods sell everything.'

" This was willingly written as a mark of friendship
for the noble young Doctor Philip de Glarges by
William Harvey, the Englishman, Physician to the
King and Professor of Anatomy.

" At London 8 May A.D. 1641."]

Nothing appears to be known of De Glarges except
that he was a wandering student of medicine,
theology, and philosophy, and an ardent collector of
autographs. He seems to have graduated at the
Hague in 1640 when he defended a thesis upon
palpitation of the heart. His collection of autographs show that he was provided with first-rate
introductions, and that he was apparently a promising student. It would be difficult, says Dr.

Aveling, to find a more suitable motto than the one Harvey has chosen to impress upon the mind of a young man. It is one which Harvey had always acted upon and found to be true.

Matters were soon brought to a crisis in England ; only four days after Harvey wrote this motto Strafford was beheaded. On January 3, 1641-2, the King's desperate attempt to seize the five members precipitated his fate. It led Parliament to make preparations for the war which had now become inevitable, and Isaac Pennington, a vigorous and determined Puritan, was chosen Lord Mayor of London. Soldiers were enrolled to form an army. On the 16th of August, 1642, the King left London, and six days later his standard was raised at Nottingham. Harvey accompanied him. The newly raised troops belonging to the Parliament, as yet ignorant of the trammels of discipline, broke into the houses of suspected persons, rifled them of their contents and often sold their booty for the merest trifle. Harvey had been living in his official lodgings at Whitehall, and though he attended the King, not only with the consent, but at the desire of the Parliament, he was very rightly suspected of being a vehement Royalist. Perhaps, too, the mention of his name in Parliament had brought him prominently into notice, for though the proceedings of the Parliament were nominally private, every act was rigorously scrutinised and actively canvassed by the agitators and local politicans. The chief outbreak of lawlessness occurred in August, 1642, immediately after it was known that the King had unfurled his standard, and it was probably on this occasion that the mob of citizen-soldiers entered Harvey's lodgings, stole his goods, and scattered his papers. The papers consisted of the records of a large number of dissections, or as they would now be called post-mortem examinations, of diseased bodies, with his observations on the development of insects, and a series of notes on comparative anatomy. Aubrey says : " He had made dissections of frogs, toads, and a number of animals, and had curious observations upon them." Harvey bitterly regretted the loss of his papers which he thus laments: " Let gentle minds forgive me, if recalling the irreparable injuries I have suffered, I here give vent to a sigh. This is the cause of my sorrow :—Whilst in attendance on His Majesty the King during our late troubles, and more than civil wars, not only with the per-mission but by the command of the Parliament, certain rapacious hands not only stripped my house of all its furniture, but, what is a subject of far greater regret to me, my enemies abstracted from my museum the fruits of many years of toil. Whence it has come to pass that many observations, particularly on the generation of insects, have perished with detriment, I venture to say, to the republic of letters."

Charles left Nottingham on the 13th of September, so that it was probably early in this month that Harvey took the opportunity of riding over to Derby to see Percival Willoughby, who had been admitted an extra-licentiate at the College of Physicians on the 20th of February, 1640-1. Willoughby says : " There came to my house at Derby, my honoured good friend Dr. Harvey. We were talking of several infirmities incident to the womb. He added to my knowledge an infirmity which he had seen in women, and he gave it the name of a honey-comb [epithelioma] which he said would cause flooding in women."

A few weeks later Harvey was actually under fire at Edgehill. The battle took place on the 23rd of October, 1642. All the morning was spent in collecting the King's troops from their scattered quarters, and it was not until one o'clock that the royal army descended the steep hill leading to the wide plain in which stand the village of Radway and the little town of Kineton. Harvey took charge of the two Princes, boys of 12 and 10 years old, who afterwards became Charles II. and James II., and in the course of the morning he probably walked along the brow of the hill from the inn at Sunrising to the Royalist head-quarters which were placed about a mile further east. Weary with waiting he and the boys betook themselves to the wide ditch at the very edge of the hill, and to while away the time Harvey took a book out of his pocket and read. " But," says Aubrey, " he had not read very long before the bullet from a great gun grazed the ground near him, which made him remove his station." As soon as the battle had really begun, Harvey, we may be sure, was alive and interested, his book was pocketed and he devoted himself at once to assist the wounded. The very nature of the wounds would give additional zest to the work for, unless he was present at the battle of Newburn-on-Tyne, this must have been his first opportunity of treating gunshot wounds. Anthony Wood in his account of Adrian Scrope shows that Harvey was no impassive spectator of the fight, for he says : " This most valiant person, who was son of Sir Jervais Scrope, did most loyally attend his Majesty at the fight of Edgehill, where receiving several wounds he was stripped and left among the dead, as a dead person there, but brought off by his son and recovered by the immortal Dr. Will. Harvey, who was there but withdrawn under a hedge with the Prince and Duke while the battle was at its height. 'Tis reported that this Adrian Scrope received 19 wounds in one battle in defence of his Majesty's cause, but whether in that fight at Edgehill I cannot justly say. Sure I am that he was made Knight of the Bath at the Coronation of King Charles II., An. 1661."

The battle was undecided, and Harvey, like the other personal attendants upon the King, must for a while have felt the keenest anxiety for the safety of his master. The King remained for a time at the top of the hill, but when the battle began in earnest he could not be restrained from mixing with the troops, sharing their danger and adjuring them to show mercy to such of the enemy as fell into their hands. Perhaps too Harvey saw one of the most picturesque acts of the battle. The Royal Standard, carried by Sir Edmund Verney at the beginning of

the fight, had waved over the King's Red Regiment
—the Royal Foot Guards. Verney slain, and the
Guards broken, it passed to the Parliamentary army,
and was committed to the charge of the secretary of
the Earl of Essex, the Commander-in-chief. Captain
Smith, a Catholic officer in the King's Life Guards,
hearing of the loss, picked up from the field the orange
scarf which marked a Parliamentarian and threw it
over his shoulders. Accompanied by some of his
troop, similarly attired, he slipped through the
ranks of the enemy, found the secretary holding
the standard, and telling him that so great a prize
was not fitly bestowed in the hands of a penman,
snatched it from him. Then, protected by the
scarf, he made his way once more through the
hostile force and laid his trophy at the feet of the
King, who knighted him upon the spot.

The battle over, Charles pushed on towards
London. Banbury surrendered on the 27th of October, and on the 29th he entered Oxford in triumph.
Harvey attended the King to Oxford where he was
at once received as a *persona grata*. His position
in London, his attachment to the King, and his
fame as a scientific man, must have combined to
render his entrance to the most exclusive Common

Rooms a matter of ease. In Oxford he very soon settled down to his accustomed pursuits, unmindful of the clatter of arms and of the constant marching and countermarching around him, for the city remained the base of operations until its surrender in July, 1646. Aubrey says that he first saw Harvey at Oxford " in 1642, after the Edgehill fight, but [I] was then too young to be acquainted with so great a doctor. I remember he came several times to our College [Trinity] to George Bathurst, B.D., who had a hen to hatch eggs in his chamber, which they opened daily to see the progress and way of generation." Two years later Bathurst was killed in defending Faringdon, but he was a distinguished Fellow of his College, and it was doubtless, with the aid and by the advice of such a friend, that Harvey was incorporated Doctor of Physic at Oxford on the 7th of December, 1642.

For the next year or two Harvey lived quietly at Oxford, making dissections and carrying on his professional work amongst the courtiers who thronged the town. It appears too from the following report that Dr. Edmund Smith was living with him in Oxford. The memorial consists of a letter from Richard Cave to Prince Rupert, concerning the health of his brother, Prince Maurice. It is preserved among the Rupert Correspondence in the British Museum, and it runs—

"May it please your Highness.

"This last night arrived here at Milton, Dr. Harvey and Doctor Smyth and this morning they were with the other two Doctors having seen and spoken with his Highness your brother intreateth me to write as followeth.

"That his sickness is the ordinary raging disease of the army, a slow fever with great dejection of strength and since last Friday he hath talked idly and slept not but very unquietly, yet the last night he began to sleep of himself and took his rest so quietly that this present morning when Doctor Harvey came to him he knew him and welcomed Doctor Smith respectively and upon Doctor Harvey's expression of his Majesty's sorrow for and great care of him he showed an humble, thankful sense thereof. Doctor Harvey asking his highness how he did, he answered that he was very weak, and he seemed to be very glad to hear of and from 'your Highness as was delivered by Doctor Harvey.

"Now the Doctors having conferred and computed

the time have good hopes of his recovery yet by reason that the disease is very dangerous and fraudulent they dare not yet give credit to this alteration. And concluding the disease to be venomous they resolved to give very little physic only a regular diet and cordial antidotes. The Doctors present their most humble service to your Highness and subscribe themselves

"Sir,

"Your Highness' most humble servants,

"WILL. HARVEY

"ROBERT VILVAIN

"EDMUND SMITH

"THO. KING.

"MILTON, *Oct.* 17th, 1643."

Dr. Aveling, from whose "Memorials of Harvey" this letter is copied, says "the treatment by 'very little phisick' and 'only a regular diet' seems to have been successful, for Cave, writing soon afterwards to Prince Rupert, says: "Maurice is not able yet to write letters, but hath this day taken physic and so intends to bid his physicians farewell."

In this year, 1643, Harvey received his last payment as physician to St. Bartholomew's Hospital. The Journals contain no record of his retirement from

office in the hospital, but the ledgers, which have been
kept with great accuracy and minuteness ever since
the granting of the Charter in 1547, show the entry
standing in its usual place, but for the last time.
"Item to Doctor Harvey, Physician, xxxiii li. vi s.
viii d." Harvey was resident in Oxford at the time
of his retirement, and the absence of any allusion
to so important an event in the history of the hospital
must be ascribed in part to the confusion of the
times. The Journals of the House of Commons,
however, contain a significant note : " Feb. 12,
an. 1643–4. A motion this day made for Dr.
Micklethwayte to be recommended to the Wardens
and Masters of St. Bartholomew's Hospital, to be
physician in the place of Dr. Harvey, who hath
withdrawn himself from his charge and is retired
to the party in arms against the Parliament." (Sir)
John Micklethwaite was as a matter of fact appointed
Physician in reversion to St. Bartholomew's Hospital,
May 26, 1648, and he succeeded to the post of full
physician May 13, 1653. He was one of the physicians in ordinary to Charles II., and died in 1682.

Harvey's presence in Oxford, and his method of
working by experiment and by logical deduction from
observation, must have been singularly agreeable to

that band of experimental philosophers who in a few years were destined to found the Royal Society. Harvey's leaven worked successfully in the brains of such men as Scarborough, Highmore, Willis, and Wren, and in due season the pupils brought forth fruit worthy of their master.

Harvey's connection with the University of Oxford was destined soon to become both intimate and honourable, though it was unfortunately only of short duration. In 1645 he was elected Warden of Merton College, in succession to Sir Nathaniel Brent. The present Warden of Merton, the Hon. G. C. Brodrick, says that on the 27th of Jan., 1645, letters were received from the King, then lodged at Christ Church, reciting that Sir Nathaniel Brent had absented himself for nearly three years, had adhered to the rebels, and had accepted the office of Judge Marshal in their ranks, to which might have been added that he had actually signed the Covenant, for he gradually became more and more Presbyterian in his views though he was originally a friend of Laud. We learn from the articles afterwards exhibited against [Sir] John Greaves, then a Fellow of the College, Savilian Professor of Astronomy, and the senior Linacre lecturer upon anatomy, that he was the person who drew up the petition against the Warden, and "in-veigled some unwary young men to subscribe to it." The King's letters accordingly pronounce the deposition of Brent, and direct the seven senior Fellows to present three persons as eligible to be his successor, out of whom the King would choose one. The Royal mandate was obeyed, but there were some irregularities in the consequent election, against which Peter Turner protested and resigned his Fellowship on his protest being overruled by Lord Hertford, who had succeeded the Earl of Pembroke as Chancellor of the University in October, 1645. However, five out of the seven seniors, including the Sub-Warden, placed Harvey first on their lists, and the King lost no time in nominating him. He was solemnly admitted Warden according to ancient custom, on the 9th of April, and two days later, on April 11th, he addressed the Fellows in a short speech which is still preserved. The extract from the College register runs :—"Dominus Custos, Convocatis in Altâ Aulâ Sociis, haec verba ad illos fecit. Forsitan decessores Custodiam Collegii ambiisse, ut exinde sese locupletarent, se vere longe alio animo nimirum ut Collegio lucro et emolumento potius foret : simulque socios, ut concordiam amicitiamque inter se colerent sedule solliciteque hortatus est." [The Warden spoke thus to the Fellows assembled in the Great Hall. He said that it was likely enough that some of his fore-runners had sought the Wardenship to enrich them-selves, but that for his own part he undertook its duties with far other motives, wishing as he did to increase the wealth and prosperity of the College. At the same time he appealed earnestly and anxiously to the Fellows to cherish amongst themselves an har-monious friendship.] The speech was thought at the time to be somewhat "Pharisaical," but there seems to be no doubt that Harvey was really expressing his feelings. There had always been a close bond between Merton and the medical profession from the days when John of Gaddesden, one of the earliest Englishmen to write a complete treatise on medicine, was a Fellow, and it was peculiarly fitting that Harvey should have been elected head of the College. He was a rich man, childless, without expensive habits, and so devoted to the pursuit of science that there is but little doubt that if he had retained his position he would have become one of the greatest benefactors of the College. As it was, the College during Harvey's year of office pre-sented more the appearance of a Court than of a seat of learning. From 1643 to 1646, when the Queen was in Oxford, she lodged in Merton College, occupying the Warden's House, and living in the room still known as " the Queen's room," with the drawing-room adjoining it. Anthony Wood says that during her occupation " there were divers marriages, christenings, and burials carefully registered in a private register by Mr. John Gurgany, one of the chaplains of Merton College ; but about the time of the surrender of Oxford the said register, among other books, was stolen by the soldiers out of his window in his chamber joining to the church door." Many officers too were quartered in Merton, and the College was so full on the 1st of August, 1645, that the annual meeting had to be held in the library, as neither the Hall nor the Warden's lodgings were available for the purpose.

The year 1645-6, during which Harvey held the office of Warden of Merton, was long a memorable one in the annals of Oxford. The City was invested by Fairfax for fifteen days from May 22nd, whilst the King was at Droitwich. On June 14th the Royal cause was ruined at Naseby, and on November 27th the College was called upon to lay in a supply of provisions against another siege. On December 28th the King ordered a special form of prayer to be used in the chapel on Wednesdays and Fridays "during these bad times." On March 24th the College gave a bond for £94 on account of provisions which it had no money to buy. At three in the morning of April 27th the King, disguised as a servant, with his beard and hair closely trimmed, passed over Magdalen bridge in apparent attendance upon Ashburnham and Hudson, and we cannot but believe that Harvey was one of the little band who closed the gates of the city with heavy hearts as his Majesty rode off to begin his wearisome captivity. On May 11, 1646, Oxford was summoned by Fairfax, and on June 24th it was surrendered on very honourable terms, the garrison marching out over Shotover 3,000 strong. The Duke of York fell into the hands of the Parliament; but Rupert, Maurice, and the greater part of the noblemen and gentlemen attendant upon the Court had left Oxford the day before its surrender. Mr. Brodrick says that " Harvey must now have retired from the Wardenship and Brent must have resumed office, though no minute of either event is preserved in the College Register. We find, however, that in September, 1648, Brent rendered accounts, as Warden, for the four years from 1642 to 1646.

Anthony Wood describes in language which has often been quoted, the utter confusion in

which the past three years had left the University
—the colleges impoverished, lectures almost abandoned, many of the students dispersed and others quite
demoralised—"in a word, scarce the face of an University left, all things being out of order and disturbed."
This account is confirmed by a striking entry in the
College Register, under the date October 19, 1646,
where it is stated that by the Divine goodness the
Civil War had at last been stayed, and the Warden
[Brent] with most of the Fellows had returned, but
that as there were no Bachelors, hardly any scholars and
few Masters, it was decided to elect but one Bursar
and one Dean. It is also added that as the Hall still
lay "situ et ruinis squalida" the College meeting was
held in the Warden's lodgings.

Of the few students whom we know that the
influence of Harvey's name attracted to Oxford that
of Charles Scarborough, the first English editor of
Euclid, is the most noted. Ejected from his fellowship
at Caius College, Cambridge, on account of his Royalist
tendencies, he immediately withdrew to Oxford, entered
himself at Merton College, obtained the friendship of
Harvey and rendered him considerable assistance in the
preparation of his work on the development of animals.
He was created a Doctor of Physic on June 23, 1646,

by virtue of letters from the Chancellor of the University, and in these letters he is described as a Master of Arts of Cambridge of seven years' standing and upwards, who was spoiled of his library in the beginning of the Civil War, and afterwards for his conscience deprived of his fellowship. His letters testimonial are under the hand of Dr. William Harvey, who says that he is well learned in Physic, Philosophy, and Mathematics.

CHAPTER VI

HARVEY'S LATER YEARS

THE surrender of Oxford in 1645 marks the period of Harvey's severance from the Court and of his practical retirement from public life. He was now 68; a martyr to gout, childless, and suffering under a series of heavy bereavements, he can have had but little heart to re-enter upon an active professional life in London. His twin brothers Matthew and Michael died in 1643. John, his second brother, died in 1645. His wife who was alive in this year, must have died shortly afterwards, or she would probably have accompanied him to Oxford. Such a series of shocks would act prejudicially upon his affectionate nature, and would still further unfit him to pursue the harassing cares of his profession. His mind, always philosophical and reflective rather than empirical, was now allowed to follow its bent to the uttermost, and his time was employed in putting into shape his treatise upon Development.

Harvey returned to London after the surrender of Oxford, and one of his first thoughts was to send to Charles Scarborough, who had continued with the Royal army, the message—" Prithee leave off thy gunning and stay here. I will bring thee into practice." And well he kept his word, for on the 8th of October, 1649, Dr. Scarborough was elected by the Company of Barber Surgeons of London reader of the anatomical lectures. "He was the first," says Wood, "that introduced geometrical and me-chanical speculations into Anatomy, and applied them in all his learned conversation, as more particularly in his famous lectures upon the muscles of the human body for sixteen or seventeen years together in the public theatre at Surgeons' Hall, which were read by him with infinite applause and admiration of all sorts of learned men in the great City. Afterwards he became a most learned and incomparable anatomist, a Fellow of the College of Physicians in 1650, principal physician to King Charles II. (from whom he received the honour of knighthood, August 15, 1669), and to His Royal Highness James, his brother, while Duke of York and when King, Physician to the

Tower of London, and afterwards to King William III." His friendship with Harvey, commenced at Oxford, continued unabated to the end of his patron's life; and when on July 28, 1656, Harvey presented to the College of Physicians the title-deeds of his paternal estate in Kent and resigned his Lumleian lectureship, the office was transferred to Charles Scarborough. In his will, too, Harvey makes affectionate mention of his friend, and bequeaths to him his surgical instruments and his velvet gown, so that literally as well as metaphorically Harvey's mantle fell upon Sir Charles Scarborough, and he nobly sustained the charge, great as it was.

The bond of friendship which had always marked the members of the Harvey family now comes into striking relief. The eldest brother, whose goods had been destroyed at Whitehall and scattered at Oxford, was a welcome guest for the rest of his life in the houses of his younger brothers. He appears to have lived chiefly at Cockaine House, which was probably situated in Broad Street, for it afterwards became the Excise Office. It was the town house of his brother Eliab, who also lived either at Roehampton or at Rolls Park. But sometimes Harvey spent a part of his time with Daniel in the suburban village of Lambeth, or at Combe, near Croydon in Surrey. Some curious details of his habits at this time have been handed down.

Aubrey says: "He was much and often troubled with the gout, and his way of cure was thus: He would sit with his legs bare, though it were frost, on the leads of Cockaine House, put them into a pail of water till he was almost dead with cold, then betake himself to his stove, and so 'twas gone." "A method of treatment," says Heberden, "which I neither recommend nor propose to others for imitation, although Harvey lived to his eightieth year, and died not so much from disease as from old age." The first coffee-house was opened in London about the year 1652 by Bowman (a coachman to Mr. Hodges, a Turkey merchant, who put him upon it), but Harvey was wont to drink coffee, which he and his brother Eliab did before coffee-houses were in fashion in London. In his will he makes a special reservation of his "coffy-pot;" his niece, Mary West, and her daughter are to have all his plate except this precious utensil, which, with the residue of his fortune, he evidently desired should descend to his brother Eliab, as a memorial doubtless of the pleasure he had often enjoyed over its contents, for coffee was not yet a common drink. Another coffee-house in London was opened just after the Restoration. It was kept by an old sergeant of Monk's army.

Among some papers at the College of Physicians relating to Harvey, which were collected by Dr. Macmichael, is one in the handwriting of Dr. Heberden, which runs as follows :—

"1761, May 29th.—Mrs. Harvey (great-niece to Dr. Harvey) told me that the Doctor lived at his brother's at Roehampton the latter part of his life. That he used to walk out in a morning, combing his hair in the fields.

"That he was humoursome and would sit down exactly at the time he had appointed for dinner whether the company was come or not. That his salt-cellar was always filled with sugar which he used to eat instead of salt.

"That if the gout was very painful to him in the night he would rise and put his feet into cold water."

This list of harmless little eccentricities is further enlarged by Aubrey, who says : "He was always very contemplative and was wont to frequent the leads of Cockaine House, which his brother Eliab had bought, having there his several stations in regard to the sun and the wind for the indulgence of his fancy; whilst at the house at Combe in Surrey, he had caves made in the ground in which he delighted in the summer-time to meditate." He also loved darkness, telling Aubrey "that he could then best contemplate." "His thoughts working would many times keep him from sleeping, in which case his way was to rise from his bed and walk about his chamber in his shirt till he was pretty cool and then return to his bed and sleep very comfortably." He was ready at all times to communicate what he knew and to instruct any that were modest and respectful to him, and when Aubrey was starting for Italy "he dictated to me what to see, what company to keep, what books to read, and how to manage my studies—in short, he bid me go to the fountain head and read Aristotle, Cicero, and Avicenna, and did call the Neoteriques" by a foul name.

Dr. Ent has left a striking picture of the old man at Christmas, 1650, nearly a year after the execution of the King. It shows at first a weariness of spirit which we would fain hope was not quite natural to him, like the sadness of age which is so marked a feature in the life-like portrait left by Janssen. Dr. Ent's account is the epistle dedicatory to Harvey's work on the development of animals, and it so clearly shows the man in the fashion as he lived, and as his beloved pupil saw him, that I have not ventured to shorten it. The Epistle is addressed :—

" To the learned and illustrious, the President and Fellows of the College of Physicians of London.

" Harassed with anxious, and in the end not much availing cares, about Christmas last, I sought to rid my spirit of the cloud that oppressed it, by a visit to that great man, the chief honour and ornament of our College, Dr. William Harvey, then dwelling not far from the city. I found him, Democritus like, busy with the study of natural things, his countenance cheerful, his mind serene, embracing all within its sphere. I forthwith saluted him and asked if all were well with him ? ' How can it be,' said he, ' whilst the Commonwealth is full of distractions, and I myself am still in the open sea ? And truly,' he continued, ' did I not find solace in my studies, and a balm for my spirit in the memory of my observations of former years, I should feel little desire for longer life. But so it has been, that this life of obscurity, this vacation from public business, which causes tedium and disgust to so many, has proved a sovereign remedy to me.'

" I, answering, said, ' I can readily account for this :

whilst most men are learned through others' wits, and under cover of a different diction and a new arrangement, vaunt themselves on things that belong to the ancients, thou ever interrogatest Nature herself concerning her mysteries.   And this line of study as it is less likely to lead into error, so is it also more fertile in enjoyment, inasmuch as each particular point examined often leads to others which had not before been surmised. You yourself, I well remember, informed me once that you had never dissected any animal—and many and many a one you have examined —but that you discovered something unexpected, something of which you were formerly uninformed.'

"'It is true,' said he ; 'the examination of the bodies of animals has always been my delight, and I have thought that we might thence not only obtain an insight into the lighter mysteries of Nature, but there perceive a kind of image or reflex of the omnipotent Creator himself. And though much has been made out by the learned men of former times, I have still thought that much more remained behind, hidden by the dusky night of nature, uninterrogated : so that I have oftentimes wondered and even laughed at those who have fancied that everything had been so consummately and absolutely investigated by an Aristotle or a Galen or some other mighty name, that nothing could by any possibility be added to their knowledge. Nature, however, is the best and most faithful interpreter of her own secrets; and what she presents, either more briefly or more obscurely in one department, that she explains more fully and clearly in another. No one indeed has ever rightly ascertained the use or function of a part who has not examined its structure, situation, connections by means of vessels and other accidents in various animals, and carefully weighed and considered all he has seen. The ancients, our authorities in science, even as their knowledge of geography was limited by the boundaries of Greece, so neither did their knowledge of animals, vegetables, and other natural objects extend beyond the confines of their country. But to us the whole earth lies open and the zeal of our travellers has made us familiar not only with other countries and the manners and customs of their inhabitants, but also with the animals, vegetables, and minerals that are met with in each. And truly there is no nation so barbarous which has not discovered something for the general good, whether led to it by accident or compelled by necessity, which had been overlooked by more civilised communities.

But shall we imagine that nothing can accrue to the wide domains of science from such advantages or that all knowledge was exhausted by the first ages of the world? If we do, the blame very certainly attaches to our indolence, nowise to nature.

"'To this there is another evil added. Many persons, wholly without experience, from the presumed veri-similitude of a previous opinion, are often led by and by to speak of it boldly, as a matter that is certainly known; whence it comes, that not only are they themselves deceived, but that they like-wise lead other incautious persons into error.'

"Discoursing in this manner and touching upon many topics besides with wonderful fluency and facility, as is his custom, I interposed by observing 'How free you yourself are from the fault you indicate all know who are acquainted with you; and this is the reason wherefore the learned world, who are aware of your unwearied industry in the study of philosophy, are eagerly looking for your farther experiments.'

"'And would you be the man,' said Harvey smiling, 'who should recommend me to quit the peaceful haven where I now pass my life and launch again upon the faithless sea? You know full well what a storm my former lucubrations raised. Much better is it oftentimes to grow wise at home and in private, than by publishing what you have amassed with infinite labour, to stir up tempests that may rob you of peace and quiet for the rest of your days.'

"'True,' said I; 'it is the usual reward of virtue to have received ill for having merited well. But the winds which raised those storms like the north-western blast, which drowns itself in its own rain, have only drawn mischief on themselves.'

"Upon this he showed me his 'Exercises on the Generation of Animals,' a work composed with vast labour and singular care, and having it in my hands I exclaimed, 'Now have I what I so much desired, and unless you consent to make this work public, I must say that you will be wanting both to your own fame and to the public usefulness. Nor let any fear of farther trouble in the matter induce you to withhold it longer; I gladly charge myself with the whole business of correcting the press.'

"Making many difficulties at first, urging among other things that his work must be held imperfect, as not containing his investigations on the generation of insects; I nevertheless prevailed at length, and he said to me, 'I intrust these papers to your care with full authority either speedily to commit them to the

press, or to suppress them till some future time.'
Having returned him many thanks, I bade him adieu
and took my leave, feeling like another Jason laden
with the golden fleece. On returning home I forthwith
proceeded to examine my prize in all its parts, and
could not but wonder with myself that such a treasure
should have lain so long concealed ; and that whilst
others produce their trifles and emptiness with much
ado, their messes twice, aye, an hundred times, heated
up, our Harvey should set so little store by his admirable observations. And indeed so often as he has sent
forth any of his discoveries to the world, he has not
comported himself like those who, when they publish,
would have us believe that an oak had spoken, and
that they had merited the rarest honours—a draught
of hen's milk at the least. Our Harvey rather seems
as though discovery were natural, a matter of ordinary
business ; though he may nevertheless have expended
infinite labour and study on his works. And we have
evidence of his singular candour in this, that he never
hostilely attacks any previous writer, but ever courteously
sets down and comments upon the opinions of each ;
and indeed he is wont to say that it is argument of an
indifferent cause when it is contended for with violence
and distemper, and that truth scarce wants an advocate.

[To face page 152.

FACSIMILE OF WILLIAM HARVEY'S HANDWRITING.

" It would have been easy for our illustrious colleague
to have woven the whole of this web from materials
of his own ; but to escape the charge of envy he has
rather chosen to take Aristotle and Fabricius of
Aquapendente as his guides, and to appear as con-
tributing but his portion to the general fabric. Of
him whose virtue, candour, and genius are so well
known to you all I shall say no more, lest I should
seem to praise to his face one whose singular worth
has exalted him beyond the reach of all praise. Of
myself I shall only say that I have done no more than
perform the midwife's office in this business, ushering
into the light this product of our colleague's genius as you
see it, consummate and complete, but long delayed and
fearing perchance some envious blast ; in other words,
I have overlooked the press ; and as our author writes
a hand which no one without practice can easily read [1]
(a thing that is common among our men of letters),
I have taken some pains to prevent the printer com-
mitting any very grave blunders through this—a point
which I observe not to have been sufficiently attended
to in the small work [2] of his which lately appeared.

[1] The kindness of Dr. Norman Moore enables me to reproduce a
facsimile of Harvey's handwriting taken from his " muscular lecture."
The block appeared originally in the *Lancet*, vol. i., 1895, p. 136.

[2] Perhaps the Essay on the Circulation of the Blood addressed to
Riolanus, published at Cambridge in 1649.

Here then, my learned friends, you have the cause of my addressing you at this time, viz., that you may know that our Harvey presents an offering to the benefit of the republic of letters, to your honour, to his own eternal fame.

> " Farewell, and prosper
>
> " GEORGE ENT."

This account brings home to us the charm of Harvey's personality. Beloved by his family and honoured by the College of Physicians, the old man went to his grave amidst the genuine grief of all who knew him. The publication of his essay on Development in 1651 was almost his last literary effort. He wrote a few letters to different friends abroad which show that his mind was still actively engaged upon the problem of the circulation of the blood, but nothing more of importance appeared from his pen. His love for the College of Physicians remained unabated, and he gave proof of it in a most practical manner. At an extraordinary Comitia held July 4, 1651, Dr. Prujean, the President, read a written paper to the assembled Fellows which contained the following proposition : "If I can procure one that will build a library and a repository for simples and rarities, such a one as shall be suitable and honourable to the

College, will you assent to have it done or no, and give me leave and such others as I shall desire to be the designers and overlookers of the work both for conveniency and ornament?" This offer from an anonymous donor was too handsome to meet with other than immediate acceptance, and as the Annals of the College express it, "super hac re prompté gratéque itum est ab omnibus in suffragia" [the proposition was instantly and thankfully agreed to by the votes of all present]. The building proceeded apace, but there is no doubt that the name of the benefactor became known, for on December 22, 1652, and before it was completed, the College voted that a statue of Harvey should be placed in their hall which then occupied a site in Amen Corner. It was accordingly erected there with an inscription upon the pedestal which ran :—

GULIELMO HARVEIO
Viro monumentis suis immortali
Hoc insuper Collegium Medicorum Londinense
posuit,
Qui enim sanguini motum
ut et
Animalibus ortum dedit,
Meruit esse
Stator perpetuus.

155

It represented Harvey in the cap and gown of his degree, and though it perished in the Great Fire of London in 1666, it was not replaced when the College was rebuilt on or near its old site nor in the more recent building in Pall Mall.

Harvey's building was a noble example of Roman architecture (of rustic work with Corinthian pilasters). It stood close to the site now occupied by Stationers' Hall, and consisted of two stories, a great parlour with a kind of convocation house for the Fellows to meet in below and a library above. This inscription was engraved upon the frieze outside the building in letters three inches long: " Suasu et cura Fran. Prujeani, Praesidis et Edmundi Smith, elect : inchoata et perfecta est haec fabrica An. Mdcliii " (This building was begun and finished in the year 1653, at the suggestion and under the eye of Francis Prujean, the President, and Edmund Smith, an Elect). Harvey therefore with characteristic modesty refrained from taking any share in the praise ; perhaps he was wise. The building is destroyed and forgotten, Smith's name has perished, Prujean's is only remembered as that of a square in the Old Bailey, but Harvey's memory remains and needs neither bricks and mortar, nor pictures, nor a statue to perpetuate it.

Harvey not only paid for the building but he furnished its library with books, amongst which were treatises on geometry, geography, astronomy, music, optics, natural history, and travels, in addition to those upon medical subjects. It was to be open on Fridays from two till five o'clock in summer, but only till four in winter; during all meetings of the College and whenever the librarian, being at leisure, should choose to be present; but no books were allowed to be taken out. The Museum contained numerous objects of curiosity and a variety of surgical instruments. The doors of the buildings were formally opened on February 2, 1653, when Harvey received the President and the Fellows at a sumptuous entertainment, and afterwards addressed a speech to them in which he made over to the College the title-deeds and his whole interest in the structure and its contents.

The College gave a fresh proof of its gratitude by choosing Harvey unanimously as its President when Dr. Prujean's term of office came to an end on Michaelmas Day, 1654. As he was absent when the election took place, the Comitia was prorogued until the next day, and Dr. Alston and Dr. Hamey, two of the Elects, were asked to wait upon him to tell him of the honour his colleagues had done themselves and him, and to say that they awaited his answer.

Every act of Harvey's public life that has come down to us is marked, as Dr. Willis very properly observes, not merely by propriety, but by grace. He attended the Comitia or assembly of the College next day, thanked his colleagues for the distinguished honour of which they had thought him worthy—the honour, as he said, of filling the foremost place amongst the physicians of England; but the concerns of the College, he proceeded, were too weighty to be entrusted to one who, like himself, was laden with years and infirm in health; and if he might be acquitted of arrogance in presuming to offer advice in such circumstances, he would say that the College could not do better than reinstate in the authority which he had just laid down their late President, Dr. Prujean, under whose prudent management and fostering care the affairs of the College had greatly prospered. This disinterested counsel had a fitting response, and Harvey's advice being adopted by general consent, Dr. Prujean was forthwith re-elected President. His first act was to nominate Harvey one of the Consilarii—an honourable office which he did not refuse to accept, and to which he was reappointed in 1655 and 1656.

That Harvey's complaint of age with its attendant infirmities was no mere figure of speech may be gathered from his letters written about this time. Thus he tells Dr. Horst, the principal physician at Hesse Darmstadt, on the 1st of February, 1654-5 : "I am much pleased to find that in spite of the long time that has passed, and the distance that separates us, you have not yet lost me from your memory, and I could wish that it lay in my power to answer all your inquiries. But indeed my age does not permit me to have this pleasure, for I am not only far stricken in years, but am afflicted with more and more indifferent health." And writing again to Dr. Horst five months later he says : "Advanced age, which unfits us for the investigation of novel subtleties, and the mind which inclines to repose after the fatigues of lengthened labours, prevent me from mixing myself up with the investigation of these new and difficult questions ; so far am I from courting the office of umpire in this dispute [about the digestion and absorption of the food] that I send you the substance of what I had formerly written about it."

Harvey appears to have devoted much of his time in his later years to a study of general literature, which must always have had many attractions to his cultivated mind—a study which is indeed absolutely necessary as a relaxation to one whose mind is bent upon the solution of obscure scientific problems if he desires to make his results intelligible. Writing to Nardi on the 30th of November, 1653, to thank him for a commentary on Lucretius' account of the plague, he goes on to say, "Nor need you plead in excuse your advanced life. I myself, though verging on my eightieth year and sorely failed in bodily health, nevertheless feel my mind still vigorous, so that I continue to give myself up to studies of this kind, especially connected with the sacred things of Apollo, for I do indeed rejoice to see learned men everywhere illustrating the republic of letters." It would seem too as if he had gained some reputation as a judge of general literature, for Howell in his familiar letters writes to him :—

"To Dr. Harvey, at St. Lawrence Pountney.

"Sir,—I remember well you pleased not only to pass a favourable censure but gave a high character of the first part of 'Dodona's Grove,' which makes this second to come and wait on you, which, I dare say, for variety and fancy, is nothing inferior to the first. It continueth an historical account of the occurrences of the times in an allegorical way, under the shadow of trees;

and I believe it omits not any material passage which happened as far as it goes. If you please to spend some of the parings of your time and fetch a walk in this Grove, you may haply find therein some recreation. And if it be true what the Ancients write of some trees, that they are fatidical, these come to foretell, at least to wish you, as the season invites me, a good New Year, according to the Italian compliment, Buon principio, miglior mezzo, ed ottimo fine. With these wishes of happiness in all the three degrees of comparison,

"I rest, Your devoted Servant,

"J. H.

"Lond. 2 *Jan.*"

As a rule it is almost impossible to fix the dates of the "Epistolæ Ho-Elianæ," but the first part of "Dodona's Grove" was issued in 1640, and the second part in 1650, so that the letter was probably written in 1651. Even if the letters were never really sent to those to whom they are addressed, Howell selected his apparent correspondents with such care that he would not have addressed Harvey in this manner unless he had been credited with some skill as a critic of general literature. This, too, is borne out in another letter to Nardi on October 25, 1655, in which he says that he is used to solace his declining years and to refresh his understanding, jaded with the trifles of everyday life, by reading the best works. Shortly before he died he was engaged in reading Oughtred's "Clavis Mathematica," and in working out the problems. The book was no doubt brought under his notice by Charles Scarborough, who with Seth Ward was the first to read it with his pupils at Cambridge, where it long remained a favourite text-book. When Scarborough and Ward were young, they once made a journey to see Oughtred, an old Etonian, "who was then living at Albury, in Surrey, to be informed of many things in his 'Clavis Mathematica,' which seemed at that time very obscure to them. Mr. Oughtred treated them with great humanity, being very much pleased to see such ingenious young men," says Anthony Wood, who tells the story, "apply themselves to those studies, and in a short time he sent them away well satisfied in their desires."

Harvey still retained his Lumleian lectureship, the duties of which he conscientiously discharged to the last. His life, says Dr. Munk, already prolonged beyond the span allotted to man, and his waning powers yet further broken by repeated and severe attacks of illness, warned him of his approaching end.

He had lived to see his grand discovery of the circulation of the blood universally accepted and inculcated as a canon in most of the medical schools of Europe; and he is said by Hobbes to have been " the only one that conquered envy in his lifetime and saw his new doctrine everywhere established." Harvey now prepared for the great change awaiting him, and on July 28, 1656, resigned his lectureship, took his leave of the College, and in so doing manifested the same zeal for its prosperity as had marked the whole of his former life. On this occasion he put the crowning act to his munificence by giving to the College in perpetuity his patrimonial estate at Burmarsh in Kent, then valued at £56 a year. The particular purposes of this donation were the institution of an annual feast, at which a Latin oration should be spoken in commemoration of the benefactors of the College, a gratuity for the orator, and a provision for the keeper of his library and museum. All this attention to perpetuate a spirit of concord and social friendship among his brethren, was in full accordance with Harvey's benevolent and liberal sentiments.

The last of his letters which has been preserved is addressed to John Vlackveld, physician at Haarlem, who had sent him an interesting specimen. The letter is a characteristic one. It runs :—

"LEARNED SIR,—Your much esteemed letter reached me safely, in which you not only exhibit your kind consideration of me, but display a singular zeal in the cultivation of our art.

" It is even so. Nature is nowhere accustomed more openly to display her secret mysteries than in cases where she shows traces of her workings apart from the beaten path ; nor is there any better way to advance the proper practice of medicine than to give our minds to the discovery of the usual law of nature, by careful investigation of cases of rarer forms of disease. For it has been found in almost all things, that what they contain of useful or of applicable, is hardly perceived unless we are deprived of them, or they become deranged in some way. The case of the plasterer to which you refer is indeed a curious one and might supply a text for a lengthened commentary by way of illustration. But it is in vain that you apply the spur to urge me, at my present age, not mature merely but declining, to gird myself for any new investigation ; for I now consider myself entitled to my discharge from duty. It will, however, always be a pleasant sight to see distinguished men like yourself engaged in this honourable arena.   Farewell, most learned sir, and whatever you do, still love

"Yours, most respectfully,

"WILLIAM HARVEY.

LONDON, *April* 24, 1657."

CHAPTER VII

HARVEY'S DEATH, BURIAL, AND EULOGY

HARVEY died at Roehampton in the house of his brother Eliab on the 3rd of June, 1657. Aubrey says that on the morning of his death, about ten o'clock, he went to speak and found that he had the dead palsy in his tongue; then he saw what was to become of him. He knew there were then no hopes of his recovery, so presently he sends for his young nephews to come up to him, to whom he gives one the minute watch with which he had made his experiments, to another his signet ring, and to another some other remembrance. He then made signs (for being seized with the dead palsy in his tongue he could not speak) to Sambroke, his apothecary in Blackfriars, to let him blood in the tongue, which did him little or no good, and so ended his days, dying in the evening of the day on which he was stricken, the palsy giving him an easy passport.

It would appear from this account that Harvey died of a cerebral hemorrhage from vessels long injured by gout and situated rather at the base or internal parts of the brain than in the frontal lobes. Most probably the left Sylvian artery gave way, leading at first to a slight extravasation of blood, which rapidly increased in quantity until it overwhelmed his brain. The copy of the death mask in the church at Hempstead shows the left eye more widely open than the right, whilst the furrows on the right side of the face are much more marked than those on the left side.

The body was brought to London, where it seems to have been placed in Cockaine House, which also belonged to Eliab Harvey, and in that room of the house which became afterwards the office of Elias Ashmole, the antiquary to whom Oxford owes the Ashmolean Museum. Here it rested many days because, though Harvey died on the 3rd of June, it was not until the 25th of June that the Fellows of the College of Physicians received a notice requesting them, clothed in their gowns, to attend the funeral on the following day. In the meantime, Eliab, as his brother's executor, had decided that

Harvey should be buried at Hempstead in Essex, and accordingly, on the 26th of June, 1657, the funeral procession started from London. It was followed far beyond the City walls by a large number of the Fellows of the College of Physicians, many of whom must afterwards have hurried back to Westminster Hall, where, on the same day, with the greatest ceremony and with all the pomp of circumstance, Cromwell was a second time inaugurated after the humble petition and advice had given him the power of nominating his successors and of forming a second House of Parliament, whilst it assigned to him a perpetual revenue.

There is no record of the time when the funeral party reached Hempstead, nor where it stopped on the way. The village is situated about fifty miles from London and seven miles east of Saffron Walden, so that one, if not two, nights must have been spent upon the journey. Here, about 1655, Eliab Harvey had built "the Harvey Chapel," a plain, rectangular building of brick with a high-pitched tile roof, on the north side of the church, adjoining and communicating with the chancel and lighted by three large windows. He had also built the outer vault beneath it as a place of sepulture for his family, and when this became full in 1766, one of his descendants, also

an Eliab Harvey, but of Claybury, built the inner vault.
Twice before had Eliab made a similar journey. Once
in 1655, after the death of his daughter Sarah, a girl of
twelve, and again in 1656, at the funeral of Elizabeth,
another daughter aged nine. Harvey was laid in the
outer chapel, between the bodies of his two nieces,
and like them he was "lapt in lead," coffinless, and
upon his breast was placed in great letters—

DOCTOR

WILLIAM + HARVEY +

DECEASED + THE + 3 +

OF + JUNE + 1657 +

AGED + 79 + YEARS.

"I was at the funeral," says Aubrey, "and helped
to carry him into the vault." The simple wrapping
of the body in lead seems to have been a custom
peculiar to the Harvey family. The leaden case
used for William Harvey was roughly shaped to the
form of the body, the head part having the rude
outline of a face with mouth, nose, and eyes; the
neck wide and the shoulders expanded. The breast-
plate was broad and the inscription upon it was in
raised letters. The body of the case was long and

tapering towards the feet, where the lead was turned up at a right angle. The measurements of the case show that it afforded no data as to Harvey's size, for though he was a man "of the lowest stature," its extreme length from the crown of the head to the toes was no less than six feet and a quarter.

When the late Sir Benjamin Ward Richardson first entered the vault in 1847, the remains of Harvey had not been visited within the memory of man, though the villagers knew by tradition that "Dr. Harvey was a very great man, who had made, they were told, some great discovery, though they did not know what it was." At that time the vault was practically open to the public, for the window in it at the eastern end was uncased and badly barred. The leaden shell containing Harvey's remains lay upon the floor just beneath the window and with the feet directed towards it. It was therefore exposed to the drift of rain when it beat into the vault with an east wind, and the sarcophagus was so unprotected that boys could throw stones upon it, and did so. The lead in the upper third of its length from the feet was almost torn through on its upper surface, though the rent was only a small one. The leaden case, too, was beginning to bend in over the middle of the body like a large scoop or spoon, in which water could accumulate.

Some repairs were made in the vault after it had been visited and its condition had been reported upon by Dr. Stewart and (Sir) Richard Quain in 1868, but the leaden case still remained upon the floor and the opening had become so large that a frog jumped out of it on one occasion as soon as it was touched. Ten years later Sir Benjamin Richardson made a further examination of the case and reported that the centre of the shell, extending from the middle of the trunk to the feet had so far collapsed that the upper surface all but touched the lower one, whilst the crack in the lead was now so large that it measured fully six inches in length. But owing to the greater collapse of the lead the fissure was not so wide as it was in 1868 ; indeed, the edges had now closed, leaving only a space of half an inch at the widest part.

" The question which interests us most," says Richardson, " has yet to be considered. Are any remains of Harvey left in the sarcophagus ? Expecting to find the opening in the lead in the same condition at my latest visit, as it was at the latest but one, I took with me a small mirror, a magnesium light, and every

appliance for making what may be called a sarcophos-
copic investigation. To my dismay, I discovered that
the opening is now almost closed by the collapse of
the lead, so that the reflector could not be used, while
the shell is positively filled at the opening with thick,
dirty fluid, like mud—a fluid thick as melted pitch
and having a peculiar organic odour. This extends
into the case above and below the crack or fissure.
There can be little remaining of the body, not much
probably even of the skeleton."

Sir Benjamin concluded his report with the suggestion that "these honoured remains should be conveyed
to their one fit and final resting-place—Westminster
Abbey. There, laid two feet deep in the floor in
some quiet corner and covered merely with a thick
glass plate, the leaden sarcophagus, still visible to
those who take an interest in the history of science,
would be protected for ages, instead of being destined,
as it now certainly is, to fall into a mere crumbling,
unrecognisable mass, in the course, at furthest, of
another hundred years." The failing health and
subsequent death of Dr. Stanley, the Dean of Westminster, prevented the execution of this project, which
would probably have been carried into effect had he
lived, for it is thought that he was willing to allow

the remains of Harvey to be placed near those of Hunter or Livingstone.

On the 28th of January, 1882, the whole tower of Hempstead Church fell towards the south-west into the churchyard. No injury was done to the Harvey Chapel, but the accident led to a further examination of Harvey's shell. It was found that the lead was perishing rapidly, and that the shell itself was full of water. A formal report was made to the College of Physicians, who appointed a committee of its Fellows to advise upon the best method of procedure. The labours of the Committee resulted in a decision to leave the remains at Hempstead, but to remove them to the chapel above the vault. The necessary consent having been obtained, and a marble sarcophagus to receive the leaden case having been selected, an architect was invited to examine the vault and the floor of the chapel. Under his directions pillars were built in the vault to sustain the additional weight upon the floor of the chapel, and on St. Luke's Day, 1883, the leaden case containing Harvey's remains was carried reverently from the vault by eight Fellows of the College. It was immediately deposited in the sarcophagus in the presence of the President, the Office Bearers, and many Fellows of the Royal College of

Physicians. A leaden case was also deposited within the sarcophagus containing the quarto edition of Harvey's works in Latin, edited in 1766 by Drs. Akenside and Lawrence, with a memorial bottle hermetically sealed and containing a scroll with the following memorial :

" The body of William Harvey lapt in lead, simply soldered, was laid without shell or enclosure of any kind in the Harvey vault of this Church of Hempstead, Essex, in June, 1657.

" In the course of time the lead enclosing the remains was, from exposure and natural decay, so seriously damaged as to endanger its preservation, rendering some repair of it the duty of those interested in the memory of the illustrious discoverer of the circulation of the Blood.

" The Royal College of Physicians, of which corporate body Harvey was a munificent Benefactor, and which by his favour is the possessor in perpetuity of his patrimonial estate at Burmarsh, Kent, did in the years 1882–83, by permission of the Representatives of the Harvey family, undertake that duty.

" In accordance with this determination the leaden mortuary chest containing the remains of Harvey was repaired, and was, as far as possible, restored to its original state, and on this 18th day of October, 1883, in the presence of four representatives of the Harvey family and of the President, all the office bearers and many other Fellows of the College of Physicians (whose names are hereunto appended), was reverently translated from the Harvey vault to this Sarcophagus, raised by the College for its reception and preservation."

High in the wall of the Church at Hempstead is a marble monument containing a bust of William Harvey. The ornamentation of the tablet is bold and effective, and below the bust is a long Latin inscription testifying to Harvey's good works. The bust was carefully examined by Mr. Thomas Woolner, R.A., who came to the conclusion that it was made from a death mask. He says that "the features presented by the bust are clearly those of a dead face. The sculptor exhibits no knowledge of sculpture except when he was copying what was directly before him. With the cast of the face for his copy he has shown true artistic delineation, but all that he has been obliged to add to make up the bust as it stands is of the worst possible quality. The ears are placed entirely out of position, the large, redundant head of hair is altogether out of character, imaginary and badly executed, and the drapery of the shoulders is simply despicable." We have nevertheless to thank the rude sculptor for the care he has devoted to the face, and we are enriched by the knowledge supplied to us by a great contemporary authority in sculpture, that the true lineaments of William Harvey, as they were seen at the time of his death, are still in our possession—lineaments which indicate a face at once refined, reflective, and commanding.

Harvey's will is an interesting document. It is without date, but it seems to have been made at some time between July, 1651, and February, 1653. The codicil is also undated. Perhaps it was added shortly before Sunday, the 28th of December, 1656, the day on which Harvey read over the whole document and formally declared and published it as his last will and testament in the presence of Heneage Finch, his nephew by marriage, afterwards the Lord Chancellor, and his faithful servant, John Raby. The will runs :

" The Last Will and Testament of William Harvey, M.D.

" In the name of the Almighty and Eternal God, Amen.

"I, WILLIAM HARVEY, of London, Doctor of Physic, do by these presents make and ordain this my last Will and testament in manner and form following, revoking hereby all former and other wills and testaments whatsoever.

"Imprimis, I do most humbly render my soul to Him that gave it and to my blessed Lord and Saviour Christ Jesus, and my body to the earth to be buried at the discretion of my executor herein after named.

"The personal estate which at the time of my decease I shall be in any way possessed of either in law or equity, be it in goods, household stuff, ready monies, debts, duties, arrearages of rents or any other ways whatsoever and whereof I shall not by this present will or by some Codicil to be hereunto annexed make a particular gift and disposition I do after my debts, funerals, and legacies paid and discharged, give and bequeath the same unto my loving brother Mr. Eliab Harvey, merchant of London, whom I make executor of this my last will and testament."

He then settles the distribution of certain lands which "I have lately purchased in Northamptonshire or thereabouts, commonly known by the name of Oxon grounds and formerly belonging unto the Earl of Manchester; and certain other grounds in Leicestershire, commonly called or known by the name of Baron Parke and sometime heretofore belonging unto Sir Henry Hastings, Knight, both which purchases were made in the name of several persons nominated and trusted by me." The will then proceeds : "And first I appoint so much money to be raised and laid out upon that building which I have already begun to erect within the College of Physicians in London as will serve to finish the same according to the design already made.

"Item, I give and bequeath unto my loving sister-in-law Mrs. Eliab Harvey one hundred pounds to buy something to keep in remembrance of me.

"Item, I give to my niece Mary Pratt all that linen, household stuff and furniture which I have at Combe, near Croydon, for the use of Will. Foulkes and to whom his keeping shall be assigned after her death or before (by) me at any time.

"Item, I give unto my niece Mary West and her daughter Amy West half the linen I shall leave at London in my chests and chambers together with all my plate excepting my coffee-pot.

"Item, I give to my loving sister Eliab all the other half of my linen which I shall leave behind me.

"Item, I give to my loving sister Daniell at Lambeth and to every one of her children severally the sum of fifty pounds.

"Item, I give to my loving cousin Mr. Heneage Finch for his pains, counsel and advice about the contriving of this my will one hundred pounds.

"Item, I give to all my little Godchildren, Nieces and Nephews severally to every one fifty pounds.

"Item, I give and bequeath to the town of Folkestone where I was born two hundred pounds to be bestowed by the advice of the Mayor thereof and my Executor for the best use of the poor.

"Item, I give to the poor of Christ Hospital [? St. Bartholomew's Hospital] in Smithfield thirty pounds.

"Item, I give to Will. Harvey my godson, the son of my brother Michael Harvey deceased, one hundred pounds and to his brother Michael fifty pounds.

"Item, I give to my nephew Tho. Cullen and his children one hundred pounds and to his brother my godson, Will. Cullen one hundred pounds.

"Item, I give to my nephew John Harvey the son of my loving brother Tho. Harvey deceased two hundred pounds.

"Item, I give to my servant John Raby, for his diligence in my service and sickness twenty pounds. And to Alice Garth, my servant, ten pounds over and above what I am already owing unto her by my bill which was her mistress's legacy.

"Item, I give among the poor children of Amy Rigdon daughter of my loving uncle Mr. Tho. Halke twenty pounds.

"Item, among other my poorest kindred one hundred pounds to be distributed at the appointment of my executor.

"Item, I give among the servants of my sister Dan at my funeralls five pounds. And likewise among the servants of my nephew Dan. Harvey at Coombe as much.

"Item, I give to my cousin Mary Tomes fifty pounds.

"Item, I give to my loving friend Mr. Prestwood one hundred pounds.

"Item, I give to every one of my loving brother Eliab his sons and daughters severally fifty pounds apiece.

"All which legacies and gifts aforesaid are chiefly to buy something to keep in remembrance of me.

"Item, I give among the servants of my brother Eliab which shall be dwelling with him at the time of my decease ten pounds.

"Furthermore, I give and bequeath unto my sister Eliab's sister Mrs. Coventrey, a widow, during her natural life the yearly rent or sum of twenty pounds.

"Item, I give to my niece Mary West during her natural life the yearly rent or sum of forty pounds.

"Item, I give for the use and behoof and better ordering of Will Foulkes for and during the term of his life unto my niece Mary Pratt the yearly rent of ten pounds, which sum if it happen my niece shall die before him I desire may be paid to them to whom his keeping shall be appointed.

"Item, I will that the twenty pounds which I yearly allow him my brother Galen Browne may be continued as a legacy from his sister during his natural life.

"Item, I will that the payments to Mr. Samuel Fenton's children out of the profits of Buckholt lease be orderly performed as my dear deceased loving wife gave order so long as that lease shall stand good.

"Item, I give unto Alice Garth during her natural life the yearly rent or sum of twenty pounds.

"Item, to John Raby during his natural life sixteen pounds yearly rent.

" All which yearly rents or sums to he paid half yearly at the two most usual feasts in the year, viz. :— Michaelmas and our Lady day without any deduction for or by reason of any manner of taxes to be anyway hereafter imposed. The first payment of all the said rents or Annuities respectively to begin at such of those feasts which shall first happen next after my decease.

"Thus I give the remainder of my lands unto my loving brother Eliab and his heirs. All my legacies and gifts &c. being performed and discharged.

"Touching my books and household stuff, pictures and apparell of which I have not already disposed I give to the College of Physicians all my books and papers and my best Persia long carpet and my blue satin embroidered cushion, one pair of brass Andirons with fire shovel and tongs of brass for the ornament of the meeting room I have erected for that purpose.

"Item, I give my velvet gown to my loving friend Mr. Doctor Scarborough desiring him and my loving friend Mr. Doctor Ent to look over those scattered remnant of my poor Library and what books, papers or rare collections they shall think fit to present to the College and the rest to be sold and with the money buy better. And for their pains I give to Mr. Doctor Ent all the presses and shelves he please to make use of and five pounds to buy him a ring to keep or wear in remembrance of me.

"And to Doctor Scarborough all my little silver instruments of surgery.

"Item, I give all my chamber furniture, tables, bed, bedding, hangings which I have at Lambeth, to my sister Dan and her daughter Sarah. And all that at London to my loving sister Eliab and her daughter or my godson Eliab as she shall appoint.

"Lastly, I desire my executor to assign over the custody of Will Fowkes after the death of my niece Mary Pratt, if she happen to die before him, unto the sister of the said William, my niece Mary West.

"Thus I have finished my last Will in three pages, two of them written with my own hand and my name subscribed to every one with my hand and seal to the last.

"WIL. HARVEY.

"Signed, sealed and ·published as the last will and testament of me William Harvey in the presence of us Edward Dering. Henneage Finch. Richard Flud. Francis Finche." A codicil is added to the will making certain rearrangements of the bequests, rendered necessary by the deaths and marriages of some of the recipients. Amongst others, "All the furniture of my chamber and all the hangings I give to my godson,

Mr. Eliab Harvey at his marriage, and all my red damask furniture and plate to my cousin Mary Harvey." "Item, I give my best velvet gown to Doctor Scarborough.

"WILL. HARVEY."

The entry of the issue of probate upon this will runs thus in the books at Somerset House :—

"May 1659. The second day was proved the will and Codicil annext of Dr. William Harvey, late of the parish of St. Peter's Poore, in London, but at Roehampton in the County of Surrey, deceased, by the oath of Eliab Harvey, the brother and sole executor, to whom administration was committed, he being first sworn truly to administer." This entry seems to set at rest the doubt that had been expressed as to the exact place of Harvey's death, for Aubrey with his customary inaccuracy in detail stated that he died in London.

William Harvey may perhaps be compared more fitly with John Hunter than with any single scientific man who either preceded or followed him. Harvey laid the foundation of modern medicine by his discovery of the circulation of the blood. Hunter laid the foundation of modern pathology, not by any single and striking discovery, but by a long course of careful observation. Harvey, like Hunter, was a careful and competent observer; both were skilled anatomists, both were ardent pathologists, both were comparative anatomists of a high order. By singular ill fortune we have lost the records of many years of careful work done by each of these great men. Harvey's work was destroyed or scattered by the violence of the times in which he lived, and we can only be grateful that so much is spared to us; Hunter's work was lost irrevocably by the crime of his trusted assistant and brother-in-law. Harvey, like Hunter, was choleric, but his nature was the more lovable, though each had the power, innate in every great teacher, of attaching to himself and enrolling in his work all sorts of unlikely people. The collecting or acquisitive spirit was equally developed both in Hunter and Harvey, but the desire for knowledge was less insatiable in Harvey.

The influence of breeding and education is nowhere more marked than in these two great men, otherwise so nearly allied. Harvey's knowledge is always well within the grasp of his intellect. He can formulate it, often in exquisite language, and it is so familiar to him that he can afford to use similes and images which show him to be a man of wide general education. He thinks clearly so that his unerring conclusions are drawn in a startlingly easy manner. Yet he was often hampered by the theories of the ancient philosophical schools of medicine. Hunter's knowledge was gigantic, but it was uncontrolled. His thoughts are obscure and so ill expressed that it is often difficult to discover what he would say. His conclusions too are sometimes incorrect and are frequently laboured, yet the advance of knowledge in the hundred years and more which separated him from Harvey afforded him many additional data.

Harvey's acquaintance with the literature of medicine enabled him to cite apposite examples, and must evidently have been of the greatest service to him in elucidating his problems. Hunter too often traversed paths which were already well trodden, for his defective education prevented him from knowing the works of his predecessors. The atmosphere of Courts and of the refined and learned society in which Harvey spent most of his life has given a polish to his writings and a gentleness to his character which were wholly wanting to John Hunter, upon whom the *res angustae domi* —absent in Harvey's case—had impressed a certain ruggedness of character, but in both there was a native strength and robustness of constitution which render them not dissimilar.

As mere practitioners or curers of the body neither Harvey nor Hunter were highly esteemed by their contemporaries, though both made considerable sums of money by their art. The curiosity both of Harvey and of Hunter was boundless, but their minds were of the creative rather than of the imaginative type. Both collected facts and were averse to theories.

Neither Hunter nor Harvey were religious men in the ordinary and narrow sense of the term. Harvey, living at an intensely religious period in the history of England, appears to have held the broad views befitting a student of nature. An eminently religious tone runs throughout his work, "a devout and reverential recognition of God," as Sir Russell Reynolds expressed it, "not only as the great primal ever-acting force, behind, outside and before all the works of Nature; but as the Being, 'the Almighty and Eternal God,' to whom he says in his last will and testament, 'I do most humbly render my soul to Him who gave it; and to my blessed Lord and Saviour Christ Jesus.'" Hunter living in a freer age had yet the remains of his Scottish upbringing adherent to the last.

CHAPTER VIII

Harvey's Anatomical Works

HARVEY'S *liber aureus* is certainly his " Exercitatio anatomica de motu cordis et sanguinis in animalibus." [An Anatomical Treatise on the Movement of the Heart and Blood in Animals, by William Harvey, the Englishman, Physician to the King and Professor of Anatomy in the London College of Physicians.] The work was issued from the press of William Fitzer, of Frankfort, in the year 1621. Harvey chose Frankfort as the place of publication for his book because the annual book fair held in the town enabled a knowledge of his work to be more rapidly spread than if it had been issued in England.

The book contains the matured account of the circulation of the blood, of which somewhat more than the germ had appeared in the notes of the Lumleian visceral lecture for 1616. It is a small quarto, containing seventy-two pages and a page and half of *errata*, for Harvey wrote a villainous hand, and communication between Germany and England was too slow, expensive, and uncertain to allow an author to correct his book sheet by sheet as it issued from the press.

The Treatise opens with a dedication to Charles I. couched in fitting emblematical language, and signed " Your Most August Majesty's Most Devoted Servant, William Harvey." The dedication is followed by a preface addressed to "Dr. Argent·[then President of the College of Physicians, and one of Harvey's intimate friends] as well as to the other learned physicians, his most esteemed colleagues." In this preface he excuses himself for the book, saying that he had already and repeatedly presented to them his new views of the movement and function of the heart in his anatomical lectures. And that he had now for nine years and more confirmed these views by multiplied demonstrations in their presence. He had illustrated them by arguments and he had freed them from objections of the most learned and skilful Anatomists. He then proceeds so modestly that it is difficult to realise how great an innovation he was really making when he says, "I profess both to learn and to teach anatomy, not from books but from dissections, not from the positions of philosophers but from the fabric of nature."

Such a statement is now a mere truism, because every one who starts upon a subject of original research follows the method adopted by Harvey. He learns thoroughly what is known already; he frames a working hypothesis and puts it to the test of experiment. He then combines his *à priori* reasoning with a logical deduction from the facts he observes. A feeble mind is sometimes overmastered by its working hypothesis, and may be led to consider it proved when a better trained observer would dismiss it for a more promising theory. Harvey's hypothesis—tested by experiment, by observation, and by reasoning—was no longer an hypothesis but a proved fact fertile beyond measure, for it rendered possible a coherent and experimental physiology and a new medicine and surgery.

The anatomical treatise gives in seventeen short chapters a perfectly clear and connected account of the action of the heart and of the movement of the blood round the body in a circle. A movement which had been foreshadowed by some of the earlier anatomists and had been clearly indicated by Harvey himself as early as 1616. But it is here laid down with a precision of detail, with a logical exactness, and with a wealth of illustration which is marvellous even to us who read of the circulation as an established and fundamental principle upon which the whole body of physic rests. Harvey's proof fell short of complete demonstration, for he had no means of showing how the smallest arteries are connected with the smallest veins. He worked, indeed, with a simple lens, but its magnifying power was too feeble to show him the arterioles and the venules, whilst the idea of an injection does not seem to have occurred to him. It was not until after the invention of the compound microscope that Leeuwenhoeck, in 1675, described the blood corpuscles and the circulation in the capillary blood vessels, though they had already been seen by Malpighi.

The first chapter of the Treatise is introductory. It is a review of the chief theories which had been held as to the uses of the heart and lungs. It had been maintained that the heart was the great centre for the production of heat. The blood was driven alternately to and from the heart, being sucked into it during the diastole and driven from it during the systole. The use of the arteries was to fan and cool the blood, as the lungs fanned and cooled the heart, for the pulse was due to an active dilatation and contraction of the arteries. During their dilatation the arteries sucked in air, and during their contraction they discharged murky vapours through pores in the flesh and skin. In the heart, as well as in the arteries, the dilatation was of greater importance than the contraction. The whole of this tissue of falsehood seems to have been founded upon an incorrect apprehension of the nature of heat. It was looked upon as a fundamental principle or entity, and until chemistry and physics reached the stage of experimental sciences it was impossible to give a correct explanation of the phenomena it presents. Even Harvey sometimes lost himself in mysticism when he had to deal with the subject of animal heat, though he was struggling hard to find a firm foothold when he said, "We are too much in the habit of worshipping names to the neglect of things. The word Blood has nothing of grandiloquence about it, for it signifies a substance which we have before our eyes and can touch; but before such titles as Spirit and Calidum Innatum [or inherent heat] we stand agape."

Harvey begins his Treatise on the movement of the Heart and Blood with the clear statement that the heart must be examined whilst it is alive ; but he says, " I found the task so truly arduous and so full of difficulties that I was almost tempted to think with Fracastorius that the movement of the heart was only to be comprehended by God. For I could neither rightly perceive at first when the systole [1] and when the diastole took place, nor when and where dilatation and contraction occurred, by reason of the rapidity of the movement, which in many animals is accomplished in the twinkling of an eye, coming and going like a flash of lightning.

" At length by using greater and daily diligence and investigation, making frequent inspection of many and various animals and collating numerous observations, I thought that I had attained to the truth . . . and that I had discovered what I so much desired— both the movement and the use of the heart and arteries. From that time I have not hesitated to expose my views upon these subjects, not only in private to my friends, but also in public in my anatomical lectures, after the manner of the Academy of old.

" These views, as usual, pleased some more, others

---

[1] The *systole* of the heart means its contraction : the *diastole* of the heart means its dilatation.

less : some chid and calumniated me and laid it to me as a crime that I had dared to depart from the precepts and opinion of all anatomists : others desired further explanations of the novelties, which they said were both worthy of consideration, and might perchance be found of signal use."

The results of his experiments soon made it plain to Harvey that the heart's movements could be studied more readily in the colder animals, such as toads, frogs, serpents, small fishes, crabs, shrimps, snails, and shellfish, than in warm-blooded animals. The movements of the heart became more distinct even in warm-blooded animals, such as the dog and hog, if the organ was attentively noted when it began to flag. The movements then became slower, the pauses longer, so that it was then much more easy to perceive and unravel what the movements really were and how often they were performed.

Careful observation and handling the heart made it clear that the organ was muscular, and that its systole was in every way comparable with the contraction which occurs in the muscles of the forearm when the fingers are moved. "The contraction of the heart is therefore of greater importance than its relaxation. During its contraction the heart becomes erect, hard, and diminished in size, so that the ventricles become smaller and are so made more apt to expel their charge of blood. Indeed, if the ventricle be pierced the blood will be projected forcibly outwards at each pulsation when the heart is tense."

After thus disproving the erroneous views of the heart's action, Harvey next proceeds to discuss the movements in the arteries as they are seen in the dissection of living animals. He shows that the pulsation of the arteries depends directly upon the contraction of the left ventricle and is due to it, whilst the contraction of the right ventricle propels its charge of blood into the pulmonary artery which is distended simultaneously with the other arteries of the body. When an artery is divided or punctured the blood is forcibly expelled from the wound at the instant when the left ventricle contracts, and when the pulmonary artery is wounded the blood spurts forth with violence when the right ventricle contracts. So also in fish, if the vessel leading from the heart to the gills be divided the blood flows out forcibly when the heart becomes tense and contracted.

These facts enabled Harvey to disprove the current theory that the heart's systole corresponded with the contraction of the arteries which then became filled with blood by a process of active dilatation, as bellows are filled with air. He illustrated this by a homely method which he had been accustomed to use in his lectures for years. He says that "the pulses of the arteries are due to the impulses of the blood from the left ventricle may be illustrated by blowing into a glove, when the whole of the fingers will be found to become distended at one and the same time and in their tension to bear some resemblance to the pulse."

The broad points in connection with the vascular system being thus settled, Harvey turned his attention more particularly to the mechanism of the heart's action. He shows that the two auricles move synchronously and that the two ventricles also contract at the same time. Hitherto it had been supposed that each cavity of the heart moved independently, so that every cardiac cycle consisted of four distinct movements. To prove that the movement of the heart was double he examined the eel, several fish, and some of the higher animals. He noticed that the ventricles would pulsate without the auricles, and that if the heart were cut into several pieces "the several parts may still be seen contracting and relaxing."

The minute accuracy of Harvey's observation is shown by his record of what is in reality a perfusion experiment. He says : " Experimenting. with a pigeon upon one occasion after the heart had wholly ceased to pulsate and the auricles too had become motionless, I kept my finger wetted with saliva and warm for a short time upon the heart and noticed that under the influence of this fomentation it recovered new strength and life, so that both ventricles and auricles pulsated, contracting and relaxing alternately, recalled as it were from death to life." We now know that this was due to the warmth, to the moisture, and to the alkalinity of Harvey's saliva, so that he performed crudely, and no doubt by accident, one of the most modern experiments to show that the heart, under suitable conditions, has the power of recovering from fatigue.

This portion of the treatise affords an insight into the enormous amount of labour which Harvey had expended in its production, for he says : "I have also observed that nearly all animals have truly a heart, not the larger creatures only and those that have red blood, but the smaller and pale-blooded ones also, such as slugs, snails, scallops, shrimps, crabs, crayfish, and many others ; nay, even in wasps, hornets, and flies

I have, with the aid of a magnifying glass and at the upper part of what is called the tail, both seen the heart pulsating and shown it to many others." That this was the result of a careful study of the animals mentioned and not a simple observation is shown by the following sentences : "In winter and the colder season, pale-blooded animals such as the snail show no pulsations : they seem rather to live after the manner of vegetables or of those other productions which are therefore designated plant animals. . . . We have a small shrimp in these countries, which is taken in the Thames and in the sea, the whole of whose body is transparent : this creature, placed in a little water, has frequently afforded myself and particular friends an opportunity of observing the movements of the heart with the greatest distinctness, the external parts of the body presenting no obstacle to our view, but the heart being perceived as though it had been seen through a window.

"I have also observed the first rudiments of the chick in the course of the fourth or fifth day of the incubation, in the guise of a little cloud, the shell having been removed and the egg immersed in clear, tepid water. In the midst of the cloudlet in question there was a bloody point so small that it disappeared during the contraction and escaped the sight, but in the relaxation it reappeared again red and like the point of a pin."

Harvey formulates in his fifth chapter the conclusions to which he had been led about the movement, action, and use of the heart. His results appear to be absolutely correct by the light of our present knowledge, and they show how much can be done by a careful observer, even though he be unassisted by any instrument of precision.

"First of all the auricle contracts, and in the course of its contraction forces the blood (which it contains in ample quantity as the head of the veins, the storehouse and cistern of the blood) into the ventricle which, being filled, the heart raises itself straightway, makes all its fibres tense, contracts the ventricles and performs a beat, by which beat it immediately sends the blood supplied to it by the auricle into the arteries. The right ventricle sends its charge into the lungs by the vessel which is called the vena arteriosa [pulmonary artery], but which in structure and function and all other respects is an artery. The left ventricle sends its charge into the aorta and through this by the arteries to the body at large.

"These two movements, one of the ventricles, the

other of the auricles, take place consecutively, but in such a manner that there is a kind of harmony or rhythm preserved between them, the two concurring in such wise that but one movement is apparent, especially in the warmer blooded animals in which the movements in question are rapid. Nor is this for any other reason than it is in a piece of machinery in which, though one wheel gives movement to another, yet all the wheels seem to move simultaneously; or in that mechanical contrivance which is adapted to firearms, where the trigger being touched, down comes the flint, strikes against the wheel, produces a spark, which falling among the powder, ignites it, upon which the flame extends, enters the barrel, causes the explosion, propels the ball, and the mark is attained— all of which incidents by reason of the celerity with which they happen, seem to take place in the twinkling of an eye. . . . Even so does it come to pass with the movements and action of the heart. . . . Whether or not the heart besides propelling the blood, giving it movement locally and distributing it to the body, adds anything else to it—heat, spirit, perfection—must be inquired into by and by, and decided upon other grounds. So much may suffice at this time, when it is shown that by the action of the heart the blood is transfused through the ventricles from the veins to the arteries and is distributed by them to all parts of the body.

"The above indeed is admitted by all, both from the structure of the heart and the arrangement and action of its valves. But still they are like persons, purblind or groping in the dark, for they give utterance to various contradictory and incoherent sentiments, delivering many things upon conjecture. . . . The great cause of doubt and error in this subject appears to me to have been the intimate connection between the heart and the lungs. When men saw both the pulmonary artery and the pulmonary veins losing themselves in the lungs, of course it became a puzzle to them to know how or by what means the right ventricle should distribute the blood to the body or the left draw it from the venae cavae. . . . . . .

"Since the intimate connection of the heart with the lungs, which is apparent in the human subject, has been the probable cause of the errors that have been committed on this point, they plainly do amiss who, pretending to speak of the parts of animals generally, as Anatomists for the most part do, confine their researches to the human body alone, and that when it is dead. They obviously do not act otherwise than he who, having studied the forms of a single common-wealth, should set about the composition of a general system of polity : or who, having taken cognisance of the nature of a single field, should imagine that he had mastered the science of agriculture ; or who, upon the ground of one particular proposition, should proceed to draw general conclusions.

" Had Anatomists only been as conversant with the dissection of the lower animals as they are with that of the human body, the matters that have hitherto kept them in a perplexity of doubt would, in my opinion, have met them freed from every kind of difficulty."

After this plea for the employment of comparative anatomy to elucidate human anatomy, Harvey proceeds to deal in a most logical manner with the various difficulties in following the course taken by the blood in passing from the vena cava to the arteries, or from the right to the left side of the heart. He begins with fish, in which the heart consists of a single ventricle, for there are no lungs. He then discusses the relationship of the parts in the embryo, and arrives at the conclusion that "in embryos, whilst the lungs are in a state of inaction, performing no function, subject to no movement any more than if they had not been present, Nature uses the two ventricles of the heart as if they formed but one for the transmission of the blood." He therefore concludes that the condition of the embryos of those animals which have lungs, whilst these organs are yet in abeyance or not employed, is the same as that of the animals which have no lungs. From this he wishes it to be understood that the blood passes by obvious and open passages from the vena cava into the aorta through the cavities of the ventricles. A statement which was in direct opposition to the generally received tradition of the time that the blood passed from the right into the left ventricle by concealed pores in the septum which separates the two cavities in the heart.

Thus far Harvey's teaching has been excellent, but now, leaving the highway of fact, he plunges into theory and is at once involved in error. He proceeds, "And now the discussion is brought to this point, that they who inquire into the ways by which the blood reaches the left ventricle of the heart and pulmonary veins from the vena cava will pursue the wisest course if they seek by dissection to discover why, in the larger and more perfect animals of mature age, Nature has rather chosen to make the blood percolate the parenchyma of the lungs, than as in other instances chosen a direct and obvious course—for I assume no other path or mode of transit can be entertained. It must be because the larger and more perfect animals are warmer, and when adult their heat greater, ignited I might say, and requiring to be damped or mitigated, that the blood is sent through the lungs, in order that it may be tempered by the air that is inspired, and prevented from boiling up and so becoming extinguished or something else of the sort. But to determine these matters and explain them satisfactorily were to enter upon a speculation in regard to the office of the lungs and the ends for which they exist. Upon such a subject, as well as upon what pertains to respiration, to the necessity and use of the air, &c., as also to the variety and diversity of organs that exist in the bodies of animals in connection with these matters, although I have made a vast number of observations, I shall not speak till I can more conveniently set them forth in a treatise apart."

The next chapter is devoted to the description of the manner in which the blood passes through the substance of the lungs from the right ventricle of the heart into the pulmonary veins. It is followed by the glorious eighth chapter, in which Harvey's style, always impressive and solid, rises into real eloquence, for a great occasion justifies the use of repetitions, of antitheses and an abundance of metaphors. He now quits the method of demonstration and experiment for that of indirect but irrefragable argument. He deals with the quantity of blood passing through the heart from the veins to the arteries, and again brings together all his threads to a nodal point. "Thus far I have spoken of the passage of the blood from the veins into the arteries, and of the manner in which it is transmitted and distributed by the action of the heart; points to which some, moved either by the authority of Galen or Columbus, or the reasonings of others, will give their adhesion. But what remains to be said upon the quantity and source of the blood which thus passes is of a character so novel and unheard of that I not only fear injury to myself from the envy of a few, but I tremble lest I have mankind at large for my enemies, so much doth wont and custom become a second nature. Doctrine once sown strikes deeply its root, and respect for antiquity influences all men. Still the die is cast, and my trust is in my love of truth and the candour of cultivated minds. And sooth to say when I surveyed my mass of evidence, whether derived from vivisections and my various reflections on them, or from the study of the ventricles of the heart and the vessels that enter into and issue from them, the symmetry and the size of these conduits, for Nature doing nothing in vain, would never have given them so large a relative size without a purpose—or from observing the arrangement and intimate structure of the valves in particular and of the other parts of the heart in general, with many things besides, I frequently and seriously bethought me and long revolved in my mind, what might be the quantity of blood which was transmitted, in how short a time its passage might be effected and the like. But not finding it possible that this could be supplied by the juices of the ingested aliment without the veins on the one hand becoming drained, and the arteries on the other getting ruptured through the excessive charge of blood, unless the blood should somehow find its way from the arteries into the veins and so return to the right side of the heart; I began to think whether there might not be a movement, as it were, in a circle. Now this I afterwards found to be true, and I finally saw that the blood, forced by the action of the left ventricle into the arteries, was distributed to the body at large and in several parts in the same manner as it is sent through the lungs impelled by the right ventricle into the pulmonary artery, and that it then passed through the veins and along the vena cava and so round to the left ventricle in the manner already indicated. This movement we may be allowed to call circular."

Harvey's great discovery is here formulated in his own words. The lesser or pulmonary circulation was already tolerably well known, owing to the work of Realdus Columbus, the successor of Vesalius in the anatomical chair at Padua, though he had been anticipated by Servetus, who published it at Lyons in 1543 in the "Christianismi Restitutio," a theological work, containing doctrines for which Calvin caused him to be burnt. But it is more than doubtful whether Harvey knew of this work, as not more than three or four copies of it have escaped the flames which consumed the book and its writer.

Harvey continues his treatise by laying down three propositions to confirm his main point that the blood circulates.

First, that the blood is incessantly transmitted by the action of the heart from the vena cava to the arteries.

Secondly, that the blood under the influence of the arterial pulse enters and is impelled in a continuous, equable, and incessant stream through every part and member of the body, in much larger quantity than is sufficient for nutrition or than the whole mass of fluids could supply.

Thirdly, that the veins return this blood incessantly to the heart. "These points being proved, I conceive it will be manifest that the blood circulates, revolves, is propelled, and then returning from the heart to the extremities, from the extremities to the heart, and thus that it performs a kind of circular movement."

These propositions Harvey proves to demonstration and in a most masterly manner. He says of the first: "Let us assume either arbitrarily or by experiment, that the quantity of the blood which the left ventricle of the heart will contain when distended to be, say two ounces, three ounces, or one ounce and a half —in the dead body I have found it to hold upwards of two ounces. Let us assume further how much less the heart will hold in the contracted than in the dilated state, and how much blood it will project into the aorta upon each contraction, and all the world allows that with the systole something is always projected . . . and let us suppose as approaching the truth that the fourth, or fifth, or sixth, or even but the eighth part of its charge is thrown into the artery at each contraction, this would give either half an ounce, or three drachms, or one drachm of blood as propelled by the heart at each pulse into the aorta, which quantity by reason of the valves at the root of the vessel can by no means return into the ventricle. Now in the course of half an hour the heart will have made more than one thousand beats, in some as many as two, three, or even four thousand. Multiplying the number of drachms by the number of pulses we shall have either one thousand half ounces, or one thousand times three drachms, or a like proportional quantity of blood, according to the amount we assume as propelled with each stroke of the heart, sent from this organ into the artery : a larger quantity in every case than is contained in the whole body. In the same way in the sheep or dog, say that but a single scruple of blood passes with each stroke of the heart, in one half hour we should have one thousand scruples, or about three pounds and a half of blood injected into the aorta, but the body of neither animal contains more than four pounds of blood, a fact which I have myself ascertained in the case of the sheep."

This is one of the highest efforts of Harvey's genius.

The facts are simple and they are easily ascertained. But the reasoning was absolutely new and the conclusion must remain sound until the end of time, for it is true. It shows too the minute care taken by Harvey not to overstate his case, for he deliberately takes a measurement of the capacity of the ventricles which he knew to be well under the average.

This part of his argument is ended with an appeal to practical experience. "The truth, indeed, presents itself obviously before us when we consider what happens in the dissection of living animals : the great artery need not be divided, but a very small branch only (as Galen even proves in regard to man), to have the whole of the blood in the body, as well that of the veins as of the arteries, drained away in the course of no long time—some half hour or less. Butchers are well aware of the fact and can bear witness to it ; for, cutting the throat of an ox and so dividing the vessels of the neck, in less than a quarter of an hour they have all the vessels bloodless—the whole mass of blood has escaped. The same thing also occasionally occurs with great rapidity in performing amputations and removing tumours in the human subject. . . . Moreover it appears . . . that the more frequently or forcibly the arteries pulsate, the more speedily will the body be exhausted of its blood during hæmorrhage. Hence also it happens that in fainting fits and in states of alarm when the heart beats more languidly and less forcibly, hæmorrhages are diminished and arrested.

"Still further, it is from this, that after death, when the heart has ceased to beat, it is impossible by dividing either the jugular or the femoral veins and arteries by any effort to force out more than one-half of the whole mass of the blood. Neither could the butcher ever bleed the carcass effectually did he neglect to cut the throat of the ox which he has knocked on the head and stunned before the heart had ceased beating."

Harvey continues to push his argument to a logical conclusion in the succeeding chapters of his Treatise partly by argument and partly by adducing fresh experimental evidence. But if any one shall here object that a large quantity may pass through (the heart) and yet no necessity be found for a circulation, that all may come from the meat and drink consumed, and quote as an illustration the abundant supply of milk in the mammæ—for a cow will give three, four, and even seven gallons a day, and a woman two or three pints whilst nursing a child or twins, which must manifestly be derived from the food consumed; it may be answered, that the heart by computation does as much and more in the course of an hour or two.

"And if not yet convinced he shall still insist, that when an artery is divided, a preternatural route is, as it were, opened, and that so the blood escapes in torrents, but that the same thing does not happen in the healthy and uninjured body when no outlet is made . . . it may be answered, that . . . in serpents and several fish by tying the veins some way below the heart, you will perceive a space between the ligature and the heart speedily to become empty, so that unless you would deny the evidence of your senses, you must needs admit the return of the blood to the heart. . . . If, on the contrary, the artery instead of the vein be compressed or tied, you will observe the part between the obstacle and the heart and the heart itself to become inordinately distended, to assume a deep purple or even livid colour, and at length to be so much oppressed with blood that you will believe it about to be choked; but the obstacle removed, all things immediately return to their natural state in colour, size, and impulse."

Harvey next proceeds to demonstrate his second proposition. He shows that the blood enters a limb by the arteries and leaves it by the veins; that the arteries are the vessels carrying the blood from the heart, and the veins the returning channels of the blood to the heart; that in the limbs and the extreme parts of the body the blood passes either immediately by anastomosis or mediately by the pores of the flesh.

Harvey is here hampered by the conditions of the age in which he lived, yet it is here that he shows himself far superior to his contemporaries as well as to the most enlightened of his predecessors. His lens was not sufficiently powerful to show him the capillary blood-vessels, and he had therefore no real knowledge of the way by which the blood passed from the arterioles into the venules. On the other hand, he did not repeat the mistake made by Aristotle, and reiterated by Cesalpino in 1571 that the blood passed from the smallest arteries into " capillamenta," the νεῦρα of Aristotle.

Later commentators have given to Cesalpino the credit due to Harvey by translating " capillamenta " into our term capillaries. But this process of "reading into" the writings of man what he never knew is one of the commonest pitfalls of defective scholarship.

Harvey attempted to solve the problem of the capillary circulation by an appeal to clinical evidence, which soon led him into inaccuracies, as when he says that the fainting often seen in cases of blood-letting is due to the "cold blood rising upwards to the heart, for fainting often supervenes in robust subjects, and mostly at the moment of undoing the fillet, as the vulgar say from the 'turning of the blood.'"

This Chapter XI. is an important one. Harvey takes the operation of bleeding as one which is familiar to every class of his readers, and he uses the various phenomena which attend the application of a ligature to the arm to clinch his arguments as to the existence of the circulation of the blood. He introduces incidentally his surgical and pathological knowledge, quoting, amongst other instances, the fact that if the blood supply to a tumour or organ be stopped, "the tissues deprived of nutriment and heat dwindle, die, and finally drop off." He also introduces some pathological results from personal experience, for he says :—"Thrown from a carriage upon one occasion, I struck my forehead a blow upon the place where a twig of the artery advances from the temple, and immediately, within the time when twenty beats could have been made, I felt a tumour the size of an egg developed, without either heat or any great pain ; the near vicinity of the artery had caused the blood to be effused into the bruised part with unusual force and velocity."

This passage shows one of the minor difficulties that Harvey and all observers in his age had to contend with in the fact that no method existed by which small fractions of time could be measured.[1] The ordinary watch had only a single hand marking the hours, so that neither minutes nor seconds could be registered by them.

The difficulty was one of old standing, and Dr. Norman Moore alluded to it, when he says in regard to Mirfeld's "Breviarium Bartholomei : " "The mixture of prayers with pharmacy seems odd

---

[1] Cardinal Nicholas de Cusa [Cusanus] is said to have counted the pulse by a clock about the middle of the sixteenth century, but Dr. Norman Moore points out to me that in reality he counted the water-clock, then in use, by the pulse. The number of pulse-beats was not measured by means of a watch until after the publication, in 1707, of Sir John Floyer's book, "The Physician's Pulse-watch, or an Essay to explain the old art of feeling the Pulse." In the time of Harvey and long afterwards physicians contented themselves with estimating the character of the pulse, rather than its precise rate.

to us; but let it be remembered that Mirfeld wrote
in a religious house, that clocks were scarce, and
that in that age and place time might not in-
appropriately be measured by the minutes required
for the repetition of so many verses of Scripture or
so many prayers. Thus Mirfeld recommends that
chronic rheumatism should be treated by rubbing
the part with olive oil. This was to be prepared
with ceremony. It was to be put into a clean
vessel while the preparer made the sign of the cross
and said the Lord's Prayer and an Ave Maria.
When the vessel was put to the fire the Psalm
'Why do the heathen rage' was to be said as far
as the verse, 'Desire of Me, and I shall give thee
the heathen for thine inheritance.' The Gloria,
Pater Noster, and Ave Maria are to be said, and
the whole gone through seven times. Which done
let that oil be kept. The time occupied I have
tried, and found to be a quarter of an hour."

In the succeeding chapters Harvey continues his
observations on phlebotomy, and draws a conclusion
so striking in its simplicity that it appears hard to
understand why it had not already occurred to
others. He says: "And now, too, we understand
why in phlebotomy we apply one ligature above

the part that is punctured, not below it : did the flow come from above, the constriction in this case would not only be of no service but would prove a positive hindrance. It would have to be applied below the orifice in order to have the flow more free did the blood descend by the veins from the superior to inferior parts."

Harvey next returns to the question whether the blood does or does not flow in a continuous stream through the heart—a subject upon which his contemporaries had the wildest notions, for even Cesalpino says : " That whilst we are awake there is a great afflux of blood and spirit to the arteries whence the passage is to the nerves and whilst we are asleep the same heat returns to the heart by the veins, not by the arteries, for the natural ingress to the heart is by the *vena cava*, not by the artery . . . so that the undulating flow of blood to the superior parts, and its ebb to the inferior parts—like Euripus—is manifest in sleeping and waking." Harvey combats this theory in exactly the same manner as we should do if it were propounded at the present day. He first brings forth his mathematical proof of the circulation, and then continues his surgical observations upon the operation of bleeding. " It is still further to be observed that in practising phlebotomy the truths contended for are sometimes confirmed in another way, for having tied up the arm properly and made the puncture duly, still, if from alarm or any other causes, a state of faintness supervenes, in which the heart always pulsates more languidly, the blood does not flow freely, but distils by drops only. The reason is that with the somewhat greater than usual resistance offered to the transit of the blood by the bandage, coupled with the weaker action of the heart and its diminished impelling power, the stream cannot make its way under the ligature ; and further, owing to the weak and languishing state of the heart, the blood is not transferred in such quantity from the veins to the arteries through the sinuses of that organ. . . . And now a contrary state of things occurring, the patient getting rid of his fear and recovering his courage, the pulse strength is increased, the arteries begin again to beat with greater force, and to drive the blood even into the part that is bound, so that the blood now springs from the puncture in the vein, and flows in a continuous stream. . . ." Thus far, he proceeds, " we have spoken of the quantity of blood passing through the heart and the lungs in the centre of the body, and in like manner from the arteries into the veins in the peripheral parts, and in the body at large. We have yet to explain, however, in what manner the blood finds its way back to the heart from the extremities by the veins, and how and in what way these are the only vessels that convey the blood from the external to the central parts ; which done, I conceive that the three fundamental propositions laid down for the circulation of the blood will be so plain, so well established, so obviously true, that they may claim general credence. Now the remaining proposition will be made sufficiently clear from the valves which are found in the cavities of the veins themselves, from the uses of these, and from experiments cognisable by the senses."

Harvey returns again to his anatomical demonstrations to prove his point. He explains the true uses of the valves in the veins, whose existence, he says, were known to his old teacher " Hieronymus Fabricius, of Aquapendente, a most skilful anatomist and venerable old man. . . . The discoverer of these valves did not rightly understand their use, nor have succeeding anatomists added anything to our knowledge ; for their office is by no means explained when we are told that it is to hinder the blood by its weight from all flowing into the inferior part ; for the edges of the valves in the jugular veins hang downwards, and are so contrived that they prevent the blood from rising upwards; the valves, in a word, do not invariably look upwards, but always towards the trunks of the veins, invariably towards the seat of the heart. Let it be added that there are no valves in the arteries, and that dogs, oxen, &c., have invariably valves at the divisions of their crural veins, in the veins that meet towards the top of the os sacrum, and in those branches which come from the haunches, in which no such effect of gravity from the erect position was to be apprehended."

"The valves are solely made and instituted lest the blood should pass from the greater into the lesser veins, and either rupture them or cause them to become varicose. . . . The delicate valves, whilst they readily open in the right direction, entirely prevent all contrary movement. . . . And this I have frequently experienced in my dissections of the veins : if I attempted to pass a probe from the trunk of the veins into one of the smaller branches, whatever care I took, I found it impossible to introduce it far any way, by reason of the valves; whilst, on the contrary, it was most easy to push it along in the opposite direction from without inwards, or from the branches towards the trunks and roots." He concludes his argument by again pointing out that the uses of the valves can be clearly shown in an arm which has been tied up for phlebotomy, and that the valves are best seen in labouring people.

The fourteenth chapter is devoted to the "Conclusion of the Demonstration of the Circulation." It runs thus :—

"And now I may be allowed to give in brief my view of the circulation of the blood, and to propose it for general adoption.

"Since all things, both argument and ocular demonstration show that the blood passes through the lungs and heart by the force of the ventricles, and is sent for distribution to all parts of the body, where it makes its way into the veins and pores of the flesh, and then flows by the veins from the circumference on every side to the centre from the lesser to the greater veins, and is by them finally discharged into the vena cava and right auricle of the heart, and this in such quantity or in such afflux and reflux, thither by the arteries, hither by the veins, as cannot possibly be supplied by the ingesta, and is much greater than can be required for mere purposes of nutrition; it is absolutely necessary to conclude that the blood in the animal body is impelled in a circle, and is in a state of ceaseless movement; that this is the act or function which the heart performs by means of its pulse, and that it is the sole and only end of the movement and contraction of the heart."

Harvey concludes his treatise with a series of reasons which he rightly considers to be of a less satisfactory nature than those he has already adduced. The seventeenth chapter contains much comparative anatomy. It opens with the statement that "I do not find the heart as a distinct and separate part in all animals; some, indeed, such as the zoophytes, have no heart. . . . Amongst the number I may instance grubs and earth-worms, and those that are engendered of putrefaction and do not preserve their species. These have no heart, as not requiring any impeller of nourishment into the extreme parts. . . . Oysters, mussels, sponges, and the whole genus of zoophytes or plant-animals have no heart, for the whole body is used as a heart, or the whole animal is heart. In a great number of animals, almost the whole tribe of insects, we cannot see distinctly by reason of the smallness of the body; still, in bees, flies, hornets, and the like we can perceive something pulsating with the help of a magnifying glass; in pediculi also the same thing may be seen, and as the body is transparent, the passage of the food through the intestines, like a black spot or stain, may be perceived by the aid of the same magnifying glass.

" But in some of the pale-blooded and colder animals, as in snails, whelks, shrimps, and shell-fish, there is a part which pulsates—a kind of vesicule or auricle without a heart—slowly, indeed, and not to be perceived except in the warmer season of the year. . . . In fishes, serpents, lizards, tortoises, frogs, and others of the same kind there is a heart present, furnished with both an auricle and a ventricle. . . . And then in regard to animals that are yet larger and warmer and more perfect, . . . these require a larger, stronger, and more fleshy heart. . . . Every animal that has lungs has two ventricles to its heart, one right, the other left, and whenever there is a right there is a left ventricle, but the contrary does not hold good ; where there is a left there is not always a right ventricle. . . . It is to be observed, however, that all this is otherwise in the embryo where there is not such a difference between the two ventricles. . . . Both ventricles also have the same office to perform, whence their equality of constitution. It is only when the lungs come to be used . . . that the difference in point of strength and other things between the two ventricles becomes apparent. In the altered circumstances the right has only to drive the blood through the lungs, whilst the left has to propel it through the whole body."

This concludes Harvey's Demonstration of the Circulation of the Blood in 1628, but he continued to work at the subject throughout his life. In two letters or anatomical disquisitions, addressed to the younger Riolanus of Paris, and dated from Cambridge in 1649, Harvey gives his latest reflections upon the subject of the Circulation of the Blood. These disquisitions differ very greatly from the original treatise. They are less clear and concise, and dwell more upon points of dispute which had arisen in connection with the controversy, which raged for many years round Harvey's discovery.

The first disquisition is devoted more especially to the question of the anastomosis which takes place between the arteries and the veins, whilst the second disquisition illustrates more fully a number of details connected with the nature and quantity of the blood and its mode of progression. Harvey says incorrectly of the anastomosis, "Neither in the liver, spleen, lungs, kidneys, nor any other viscus, is such a thing as an anastomosis to be seen, and by boiling I have rendered the whole parenchyma of these organs so friable that it could be shaken like dust from the fibres or picked away with a needle, until I could trace the fibres of every sub-division, and see every capillary filament distinctly. I can, therefore, boldly affirm that there is neither any anastomosis of the vena portæ with the cava, of the arteries with the veins, or of the capillary ramifications of the biliary ducts, which can be traced through the entire liver, with the veins."

The second disquisition opens with Harvey's view of the contemporary criticism upon his treatise. "But scarce a day, scarce an hour has passed since the birth-day of the Circulation of the blood that I have not heard something, for good or for evil, said of this, my discovery. Some abuse it as a feeble infant, and yet unworthy to have seen the light ; others again think the bantling deserves to be cherished and càred for. These oppose it with much ado, those patronise it with abundant commendation. One party holds that I have completely demonstrated the circulation of the blood by experiment, observation, and ocular inspection against all force and array of argument ; another thinks it scarcely sufficiently illustrated — not yet cleared of all objections. There are some, too, who say that I have shown a vainglorious love of vivisections, and who scoff at and deride the introduction of frogs and serpents, flies, and other of the lower animals upon the scene, as a piece of puerile levity, not even refraining from opprobrious epithets.

"To return evil speaking with evil speaking, however, I hold to be unworthy in a philosopher and searcher after truth. I believe that I shall do better and more advisedly if I meet so many indications of ill breeding with the light of faithful and conclusive observation. It cannot be helped that dogs bark and vomit their foul stomachs, or that cynics should be numbered among philosophers ; but care can be taken that they do not bite or inoculate their mad humours, or with their dogs' teeth gnaw the bones and foundations of truth.

" Detractors, mummers, and writers defiled with abuse, as I resolved with myself never to read them, satisfied that nothing solid or excellent, nothing but foul terms was to be expected from them, so have I held them still less worthy of an answer. Let them consume on their own ill-nature. They will scarcely find many well-disposed readers, I imagine, nor does God give that which is most excellent, and chiefly to be desired—wisdom—to the wicked. Let them go on railing, I say, until they are weary, if not ashamed."

Amidst a mass of unprofitable speculation, the second Disquisition contains one or two gems of pathological observation, illustrating physiological conclusions. Desiring to set in a clear light "that the pulsific power does not proceed from the heart by the coats of the vessels, I beg here to refer to a portion of the descending aorta, about a span long in length, with its division into two crural trunks, which I removed from the body of a nobleman, and which is converted into a bony tube: by this hollow tube nevertheless, did the arterial blood reach the lower extremities of this nobleman during his life, and cause the arteries in these to beat . . . . Where it was converted into bone it could neither dilate nor contract like bellows, nor transmit the pulsific power from the heart to the inferior vessels: it could not convey a force which it was incapable of receiving through the solid matter of the bone. In spite of all, however, I well remember to have frequently noticed the pulse in the legs and feet of this patient whilst he lived, for I was myself his most attentive physician, and he my very particular friend. The arteries in the inferior extremities of this nobleman must, therefore, and of necessity, have been dilated by the impulse of the bloodlike flaccid sacs, and not have expanded in the manner of bellows through the action of their tunics.

"I have several times opened the breast and pericardium of a man within two hours after his execution by hanging, and before the colour had totally left his face, and in presence of many witnesses, have demonstrated the right auricle of the heart and the lungs distended with blood : the auricle in particular of the size of a large man's fist, and so full of blood that it looked as if it would burst. This great distension, however, had disappeared next day, the body having stiffened and become cold, and the blood having made its escape through various channels.

"I add another observation. A noble knight, Sir Robert Darcy, an ancestor of that celebrated physician and most learned man, my very dear friend, Dr. Argent, when he had reached to about the middle period of life, made frequent complaint of a certain distressing pain in the chest, especially in the night season, so that dreading at one time syncope, at another suffocation in his attacks, he led an unquiet and anxious life. He tried many remedies in vain, having had the advice of almost every medical man. The disease going on from bad to worse, he by and by became cachectic and dropsical, and finally grievously distressed, he died in one of his paroxysms. In the body of this gentleman, at the inspection of which there were present Dr. Argent, the President of the College of Physicians, and Dr. Gorge, a distinguished theologian and preacher, who was pastor of the parish, we found the wall of the left ventricle of the heart ruptured, having a rent in it of size sufficient to admit any of my fingers, although the wall itself appeared sufficiently thick and strong. This laceration had apparently been caused by an impediment to the passage of the blood from the left ventricle into the arteries.

"I was acquainted with another strong man, who, having received an injury and affront from one more powerful than himself, and upon whom he could not have his revenge, was so overcome with hatred and spite and passion, which he yet communicated to no one, that at last he fell into a strange distemper, suffering from extreme oppression and pain of the heart and breast, and the prescriptions of none of the very best physicians proving of any avail, he fell in the course of a few years into a scorbutic and cachectic state, became tabid, and died. This patient only received some little relief when the whole of his chest was pummelled or kneaded by a strong man, as a baker kneads dough. His friends thought him poisoned by some maleficent influence or possessed with an evil spirit. His jugular arteries enlarged to the size of a thumb, looked like the aorta itself, or they were as large as the descending aorta : they had pulsated violently and appeared like two long aneurysms. These symptons had led to trying the affects of arteriotomy in the temples, but with no relief. In the dead body I found the heart and aorta so much gorged and distended with blood that the cavities of the ventricles equalled those of a bullock's heart in size. Such is the force of the blood pent up, and such are the effects of its impulse."

His letters show that Harvey was employed almost to the end of his life in devising fresh experiments in proof of the circulation of the blood. Thus, in a letter addressed to Paul Marquard Slegel, and dated London, this 26th of March, 1651, Harvey writes : " It may be well here to relate an experiment which I lately tried in the presence of several of my colleagues. . . . Having tied the pulmonary artery, the pulmonary veins, and the aorta, in the body of a man who had been hanged, and then opened the left ventricle of the heart, we passed a tube through the vena cava into the right ventricle of the heart, and having at the same time attached an ox's bladder to the tube, in the same way as a clyster-bag is usually made, we filled it nearly full of warm water and forcibly injected the fluid into the heart, so that the greater part of a pound of water was thrown into the right auricle and ventricle. The result was that the right ventricle and auricle were enormously distended, but not a drop of water or of blood made its escape through the orifice in the left ventricle. The ligatures having been undone, the same tube was passed into the pulmonary artery and a tight ligature having been put round it to prevent any reflux into the right ventricle, the water in the bladder was now pushed towards the lungs, upon which a torrent of the fluid, mixed with a quantity of blood, immediately gushed forth from the perforation in the left ventricle: so that a quantity of water, equal to that which was pressed from the bladder into the lungs at each effort, instantly escaped by the perforation mentioned. You may try this experiment as often as you please : the result you will still find to be as I have stated it."

The exact teaching of Harvey's contemporaries in London is easily accessible. One of his distinguished colleagues at the College of Physicians was Alexander Reid, son of the first minister of Banchory, near

Aberdeen, brother of Thomas Reid, Secretary for Latin and Greek to King James I. Reid was born about 1586, learnt Surgery in France, was admitted a Fellow of the College of Physicians in 1624, and was appointed Lecturer on Anatomy at the Barber Surgeons' Hall December 28, 1628, in succession to Dr. Andrewes, Harvey's assistant. Reid, eight years younger than Harvey, lectured at an annual stipend of £20 on every Tuesday throughout the year from 1628 to 1634, when he published a tiny Manual of Anatomy containing the substance of his lectures. For some reason Harvey's doctrines did not recommend themselves to Reid, and the Manual therefore contains the following traditional account of the heart.

"As for the heart, the substance of it is compact and firm, and full of fibres of all sorts. The upper part is called *Basis* or *Caput* : the lower part *Conus*, *Mucro* or *Apex Cordis*. When the heart contracteth itself it is longer, and so the point is drawn from the head of it. But when it dilateth itself it becometh rounder, the conus being drawn to the basis. About the basis the fat is. It is covered with a skin which hardly can be separat[ed]. In moist and cowardly creatures, it is biggest . . . . Of all parts of the body it is hottest, for it is the wellspring of life, and by arteries communicateth it to the rest of the body. The heart hath two motions, Diastole and Systole. In Diastole, or dilatation of the heart, the conus is drawn from the basis to draw blood by the cava to the right ventricle, and air by the arteria venosa [pulmonary vein] to the left ventricle. In Systole or contraction the conus is drawn to the basis.

"First, that the vital spirit may be thrust from the left ventricle of the heart into the aorta.

"Secondly, that the arterial blood may be thrust into the lungs by arteria venalis [the left auricle].

"Thirdly, that the blood may be pressed to the lungs, in the right ventricle by vena arterialis [right auricle].

"The septum so called because it separateth the right ventricle from the left, is that thick and fleshy substance set between the two cavities.

"Riolan will have it the matter of the vital blood to pass through the holes or porosities of it from the right to the left ventricle, but that hardly any instrument can show them. First, because they go not straight, but wreathed. Secondly, because they are exceeding narrow in the end. He affirmeth that they are more easily discerned in an ox-heart boiled."

It is difficult to realise how any reasonable man could teach such a farrago of nonsense when he must have heard Harvey's perfectly simple and clear demonstration of the structure and uses of the heart. Harvey was lecturing on Tuesdays, Wednesdays, and Thursdays ; Reid only lectured on Tuesdays, and Harvey had especially set himself to controvert the very errors that Reid was promulgating. But Reid was perfectly impenitent, for his Manual was reprinted in 1637, in 1638 ; and after his death it appeared again in 1642, 1650, 1653, and 1658, yet there is no alteration in his text. He was not even sure of the broad features of the anatomy of the heart, for he writes : " The first vessel in the chest is the vena cava or magna. The second vessel in the breast is vena arterialis. It is a vein from its office, for it carrieth natural blood to the lungs by the right side of the windpipe. It is called an artery because the coat of it is double, not single. It doth spring from the upper part of the right ventricle of the heart, and is implanted into the substance of the lungs by the right side of the windpipe."

It seems obvious that this is a perverted description of the right auricle, and that Reid had no idea of the pulmonary artery as a distinct structure.

"The third vessel is arteria venalis. It is called an artery because it carrieth arterial blood, but a vein because it hath a single coat as a vein. It ariseth from the upper part of the left ventricle of the heart, and is implanted into the substance of the lungs by the left side of the windpipe."

This in like manner appears to be the left auricle and the pulmonary veins.

"The vena arterialis hath three valves called sigmoides from the figure of the great sigma, which answereth the Latin S, the figure is this, C. They look from within outwards, to let out the blood but to hinder the return of the same.

"The arteria venalis hath two valves called mitrales, because they are like a bishop's mitre. They look from without inward to let in blood carried from the vena arterialis. They are bigger than those of vena cava and have longer filaments and to strengthen them many fleshy snippets are joined together.

"It hath two valves only that the fuliginous vapours might the more readily be discharged."

Reid, like all his contemporaries, had a glimmering of the lesser circulation, for he says : "First the blood is carried by vena arterialis and from hence to arteria venalis by sundry anastomoses, and from hence to the left ventricle of the heart. Where being made spirituous it is sent by the aorta to impart life to the whole body.

"One thing is to be noted that no air in its proper substance is carried to the heart ; for the blood contained in these two vessels is sufficiently cooled by the bronchia passing between them. . . . One thing is to be noted, that in arteria venosa a little below the valves there is found a little valve ever open. It being removed, there appeareth a hole by the which the blood passeth freely from the vena cava to it and returneth by reason of this anastomosis that the blood in the veins may be animate." This is a description of the foramen ovale and its use.

Such a comparison with the work of a contemporary teacher in the same town shows how immeasurable was the advance made by Harvey. It only remains to show what has been done since his death to perfect our knowledge of the heart and of the circulation. The use of the microscope by Malpighi in 1661 gave an insight into the true nature of the porosities by which the blood passed from the terminal arteries to the commencing veins in the lungs and proved them to be vessels. The capillary circulation was still further investigated by Leeuwenhoek in 1674 who described it as it is seen in the web of a frog's foot, and in other transparent membranes; Blankaart in 1676, William Cowper in 1697, and afterwards Ruysch, studied the arrangement of the capillaries by means of injection. In 1664 Stenson demonstrated that the heart was a purely muscular organ.

The various histological details being thus settled there came a long interval until chemistry was sufficiently advanced to enable definite statements to be made about the aëration of the blood.

The work of Black in 1757 and of Priestley and others in 1774 and 1775 at last allowed the process of respiration and the true function of the lungs to be explained upon scientific grounds. But the interval between the discovery of the capillaries and the explanation of the act of respiration was not wholly barren; for in 1732 Archdeacon Hales, by means of experiments, obtained an important insight into the hydraulics of the circulation. During the present century our knowledge of the physics of the heart and circulation has been reduced almost to an exact science by the labours of the German, French, and Cambridge schools of physiology under the guidance respectively of Ludwig, of Chauveau, and of Foster; whilst the nervous mechanism of the heart and of the arteries has been thoroughly investigated by Gaskell and others.

CHAPTER IX

THE TREATISE ON DEVELOPMENT

FULLER, speaking of Harvey, says very ingeniously : "The Doctor though living a Bachelor, may be said to have left three hopeful sons to posterity : his books,

"1. De circulatione sanguinis, which I may call his son and heir : the Doctor living to see it at full age and generally received.

"2. De generatione, as yet in its minority : but I assure you growing up apace into public credit.

"3. De ovo, as yet in the nonage thereof; but infants may be men in due time."

The treatises on Development are so full of detail that it is impossible to give an exact notion of their contents in a popular work. They contain however certain passages of personal and of general interest which must not be omitted.

Harvey shows the instinct of a naturalist in the following account of the cassowary which was not only new to him, but was unknown to Europe at the time he wrote. He says : " A certain bird, as large again as a swan, which the Dutch call a cassowary, was imported no long time ago from the island of Java in the East Indies into Holland. Ulysses Aldrovandus gives a figure of this bird and informs us that it is called an emu by the Indians. It is not a two-toed bird like the ostrich but has three toes on each foot, one of which is furnished with a spur of such length, strength, and hardness that the creature can easily kick through a board two fingers' breadth in thickness. The cassowary defends itself by kicking forwards. In the body, legs, and thighs it resembles the ostrich : it has not a broad bill like the ostrich, however, but one that is rounded and black. On its head by way of crest it has an orbicular protuberant horn. It has no tongue and devours everything that is presented to it—stones, coals even though alight, pieces of glass—all without distinction. Its feathers sprout in pairs from each particular quill and are of a black colour, short and slender, and approaching to hair or down in their character. Its wings are very short and imperfect. The whole aspect of the creature is truculent, and it has numbers of red and blue wattles longitudinally disposed along the neck.

"This bird remained for more than seven years in Holland and was then sent among other presents by the illustrious Maurice Prince of Orange to his Serene Majesty, our King James, in whose gardens it continued to live for a period of upwards of five years."

It has already been shown that Harvey was on a footing of something like intimacy with his master the King, whose artistic and scientific tastes are well known. This fact is again made clear by the following passages, in which Harvey followed his usual custom of showing to the King anything unusually curious. "I have seen a very small egg covered with a shell, contained within another larger egg, perfect in all respects and completely surrounded with a shell. An egg of this kind Fabricius calls an ovum centennium, and our housewives ascribe it to the cock. This egg I showed to his Serene Majesty King Charles, my most gracious master, in the presence of many persons. And the same year, in cutting up a large lemon, I found another perfect but very small lemon included within it, having a yellow rind like the other, and I hear that the same thing has frequently been seen in Italy." Speaking in another place of these eggs, he says: " Some eggs too are larger, others smaller ; a few extremely small. These in Italy are commonly called centennia, and our country folks still believe that such eggs are laid by the cock, and that were they set they would produce basilisks. ' The vulgar,' says Fabricius, ' think that this small egg is the last that will be laid and that it comes as the hundredth in number, whence the name ; that it has no yolk, though all the other parts are present—the chalazae, the albumen, the membranes, and the shell.'

" It was customary with his Serene Majesty, King Charles, after he had come to man's estate, to take the diversion of hunting almost every week, both for the sake of finding relaxation from graver cares and for his health. The chase was principally the buck and doe, and no prince in the world had greater herds of deer, either wandering in freedom through the wilds and forests or kept in parks and chases for this purpose. The game, during the three summer months, was the buck then fat and in season ; and in the autumn and winter for the same length of time the doe. This gave me an opportunity of dissecting numbers of these animals almost every day during the whole of the season. . . . I had occasion, so often as I desired it, to examine and study all the parts . . . because the great prince, whose physician I was, besides taking much pleasure in such inquiries and not disdaining to bear witness to my discoveries, was pleased in his kindness and munificence to order me an abundant supply of these animals, and repeated opportunities of examining their bodies." Speaking of the first rudiments of the heart, he says : " I have exhibited this point to his Serene Highness the King, still palpitating. . . . It was extremely minute indeed, and without the advantage of the sun's light falling upon it from the side, its tremulous motions were not to be perceived."

The late Sir George Paget published, in 1850, an autograph letter from Dr. Ward the learned divine and stout-hearted Royalist, who was master of Sidney Sussex College, Cambridge, from 1609 to 1643. Both the letter and Harvey's reply show the interest taken by King Charles in such scientific curiosities ; but Harvey's letter is also valuable because the peculiarities of its writing and annotation led to the discovery that the manuscript lectures in the British Museum [pp. 52–69] were in the handwriting of Harvey. It must, therefore, be looked upon as the origin of most of the recently acquired knowledge of the discoverer of the circulation of the blood, of his methods of observation, of his reading, and of his system of arrangement, and of verbal exposition.

Dr. Ward's letter is as follows :—

" SIR,—I received your letter by which I understand his Majesty's pleasure that I should send up the petrified skull, which we have in our College Library, which accordingly I have done, with the case wherein we keep it.   And I send in this letter both the key of the case and a note which we have recorded of the Donor and whence he had it.   And so with my affectionate prayers and best devotions for the long life of his sacred Majesty and my service to yourself I rest

" At Your Command,

" SAMUEL WARD.

"SIDNEY COLLEGE, *June* 10, *Sunday*."

The address is—

" To his much honoured friend Doctor Harvey one of his Majesty's Physicians at his house in the Blackfriars be this delivered."

243

The following is Harvey's reply ; it is written on the back of Dr. Ward's letter :—

" Mr. Doctor Ward, I have showed to his Majesty this skull incrustated with stone which I received from you, and his Majesty wondered at it and looked content to see so rare a thing. I do now with thanks return it to you and your College, the same with the key of the case and the memorial you sent me enclosed herein, thinking it a kind of sacrilege not to have returned it to that place where it may for the instruction of men hereafter be conserved." ·

The letter and skull have been preserved in a small ancient cabinet of carved oak, which stands in the Library of Sidney College. The skull is very curious. It is that of a young person and is encrusted with carbonate of lime, which is very hard and compact and is spread over the bone in such a manner as to resemble a petrification of the soft parts. The "note of the Donour" states that he was Captain William Stevens of Rotherhithe, one of the elder brethren of the Trinity, and that he brought the skull in 1627 from Crete where it was discovered about ten yards (circiter passus decem) below the surface of the ground in digging a well near the town of Candia.

Harvey's pathological knowledge was sometimes called into use by the King as in the following case :—
" A young nobleman, eldest son of the Viscount Montgomery,[1] when a child, had a severe fall attended with fracture of the ribs of the left side. The consequence of this was a suppurating abscess, which went on discharging abundantly for a long time, from an immense gap in his side : this I had from himself and other credible persons who were witnesses. Between the eighteenth and nineteenth years of his age, this young nobleman having travelled through France and Italy, came to London, having at this time a very large open cavity in his side, through which the lungs as it was believed could both be seen and touched. When this circumstance was told as something miraculous to his Serene Majesty King Charles, he straightway sent me to wait upon the young man, that I might ascertain the true state of the case. And what did I find ? A young man, well grown, of good complexion and apparently possessed of an excellent constitution, so that I thought the whole story must be a fable. Having saluted him according to custom, however,

[1] Dr. Norman Moore suggests that this young nobleman was possibly Philip Herbert (d. 1669), son of Philip Herbert, the second son of Henry, Earl of Pembroke (d. 1648), created Earl of Montgomery 1605–6, and Lord Chamberlain.

and informed him of the King's expressed desire that I should wait. upon him, he immediately showed me everything, and laid open his left side for my inspection, by removing a plate which he wore there by way of defence against accidental blows and other external injuries. I found a large open space in the chest, into which I could readily introduce three of my fingers and my thumb : which done, I straightway perceived a certain protuberant fleshy part, affected with an alternating extrusive and intrusive movement : this part I touched gently. Amazed with the novelty of such a state, I examined everything again and again, and when I had satisfied myself, I saw that it was a case of old and extensive ulcer, beyond the reach of art, but brought by a miracle to a kind of cure, the interior being invested with a membrane and the edges protected with a tough skin. But the fleshy part (which I at first sight took for a mass of granulations, and others had always regarded as a portion of the lung) from its pulsating motions and the rhythm they observed with the pulse—when the fingers of one of my hands were applied to it, those of the other to the artery at the wrist—as well as from their discordance with the respiratory movements, I saw was no portion of the lung that I was handling, but the apex of the heart! covered over with a layer of fungous flesh by way of external defence as commonly happens in old foul ulcers. The servant of this young man was in the habit daily of cleansing the cavity from its accumulated sordes by means of injections of tepid water : after which the plate was applied, and with this in its place, the young man felt adequate to any exercise or expedition, and in short he led a pleasant life in perfect safety.

"Instead of a verbal answer, therefore, I carried the young man himself to the King, that his Majesty might with his own eyes behold this wonderful case : that, in a man alive and well, he might without detriment to the individual, observe the movement of the heart, and with his own hand even touch the ventricles as they contracted. And his most excellent Majesty, as well as myself, acknowledged that the heart was without the sense of touch : for the youth never knew when we touched his heart, except by the sight or sensation he had through the external integument.

"We also particularly observed the movements of the heart, viz., that in the diastole it was retracted and withdrawn : whilst in the systole it emerged and protruded : and the systole of the heart took place at the moment the diastole or pulse in the wrist was perceived ; to conclude, the heart struck the walls of the chest and became prominent at the time it bounded upwards and underwent contraction on itself."

Harvey's powers of observation were particularly brought into play in connection with his experiments on the development of the chick. He fully appreciated the method of Zadig, for he says that " different hens lay eggs that differ much in respect of size and figure, some habitually lay more oblong, others rounder eggs that do not differ greatly from one another : and although I sometimes found diversities in the eggs of the same fowl, these were still so trifling in amount that they would have escaped any other than the practised eye . . . so that I myself, without much experience, could readily tell which hen in a small flock had laid a given egg and that they who have given much attention to the point of course succeed much better. But that which we note every day among huntsmen is far more remarkable : for the more careful keepers who have large herds of stags or fallow deer under their charge, will very certainly tell to which herd the horns they find in the woods or thickets belonged. A stupid and uneducated shepherd, having the charge of a numerous flock of sheep, has been known to become so familiar with the physiognomy of each, that if any one had strayed from the flock though he could not count them, he

could still say which one it was, give the particulars as
to where it had been bought or whence it had come.
The master of this man for the sake of trying him,
once selected a particular lamb from among forty others
in the same pen and desired him to carry it to the ewe
which was its dam, which he did forthwith. We
have known huntsmen who having only once seen a
particular stag or his horns or even his print in the
mud (as a lion is known by his claws) have afterwards
been able to distinguish him by the same marks from
every other. Some, too, from the footprints of deer,
seen for the first time, will draw inferences as to the
size and grease and power of the stag which has left
them : saying whether he were full of strength or
weary from having been hunted, and farther whether
the prints are those of a buck or doe. I shall say this
much more, there are some who in hunting, when
there are some forty hounds upon the trace of the
game and all are giving tongue together will nevertheless, and from a distance, tell which dog is at the
head of the pack, which at the tail, which chases on
the hot scent, which is running off at fault, whether
the game is still running or at bay, whether the stag
have run far or have but just been raised from his lair.
And all this amid the din of dogs and men and horns

and surrounded by an unknown and gloomy wood. We should not therefore be greatly surprised when we see those who have experience telling by what hen each particular egg in a number has been laid. I wish there was some equally ready way from the child of knowing the true father."

The next extract gives a good example of Harvey's general style. Speaking of the escape of the chicken from the egg, he says : " Now we must not overlook a mistake of Fabricius and almost every one else in regard to this exclusion or birth of the chick. Let us hear Fabricius.

" ' The chick wants air sooner than food, for it has still some store of nourishment within it : in which case the chick by his chirping gives a sign to his mother of the necessity of breaking the shell, which he himself cannot accomplish by reason of the hardness of the shell and the softness of his beak, to say nothing of the distance of the shell from the beak and of the position of the head under the wing. The chick, nevertheless, is already so strong, and the cavity in the egg is so ample, and the air contained within it so abundant, that the breathing becomes free and the creature can emit the sounds that are proper to it. These can be readily heard by a bystander, and were recognised both by Pliny and Aristotle, and perchance have something of the nature of a petition in their tone. For the hen hearing the chirping of the chick within, and knowing thereby the necessity of now breaking the shell in order that the chick may enjoy the air which has become needful to it, or if you will, you may say, that desiring to see her dear offspring, she breaks the shell with her beak, which is not hard to do, for the part over the hollow long deprived of moisture and exposed to the heat of incubation, has become dry and brittle. The chirping of the chick is consequently the first and principal indication of the creature desiring to make its escape and of its requiring air. This the hen perceives so nicely, that if she hears the chirping to be low and internal, she straight-way turns the egg over with her feet, that she may break the shell at the place whence the voice proceeds without detriment to the chick.' Hippocrates adds, ' Another indication or reason of the chick's desiring to escape from the shell, is that when it wants food it moves vigorously, in search of a larger supply, by which the membrane around it is torn, and the mother breaking the shell at the place where she hears the chick moving most lustily, permits it to escape.'

"All this is stated pleasantly and well by Fabricius ;

but there is nothing of solid reason in the tale. For I have found by experience that it is the chick himself and not the hen that breaks open the shell, and this fact is every way in conformity with reason. For how else should the eggs which are hatched in dung-hills and ovens, as in Egypt and other countries, be broken in due season, where there is no mother present to attend to the voice of the supplicating chick and to bring assistance to the petitioner ? And how again are the eggs of sea and land tortoises, of fishes, silkworms, serpents, and even ostriches to be chipped ? The embryos in these have either no voice with which they can notify their desire for deliverance, or the eggs are buried in the sand or slime where no chirping or noise could be heard. The chick, therefore, is born spontaneously, and makes its escape from the eggshell through its own efforts. That this is the case appears from unquestionable arguments : when the shell is first chipped the opening is much smaller than accords with the beak of the mother, but it corresponds exactly to the size of the bill of the chick, and you may always see the shell chipped at the same distance from the extremity of the egg and the broken pieces, especially those that yield to the first blows, projecting regularly outwards in the form of a circlet. But as any one on looking at a broken pane of glass can readily determine whether the force came from without or from within by the direction of the fragments that still adhere, so in the chipped egg it is easy to perceive, by the projection of the pieces around the entire circlet, that the breaking force comes from within. And I myself, and many others with me besides, hearing the chick scraping against the shell with its feet, have actually seen it perforate this part with its beak and extend the fracture in a circle like a coronet. I have further seen the chick raise up the top of the shell upon its head and remove it.

"We have gone at length into some of these matters, as thinking that they were not without all speculative interest, as we shall show by and by. The arguments of Fabricius are easily answered. For I admit that the chick produces sounds whilst it is still within the egg, and these perchance may even have something of the implorative in their nature : but it does not therefore follow that the shell is broken by the mother. Neither is the bill of the chick so soft, nor yet so far from the shell, that it cannot pierce through its prison walls, particularly when we see that the shell, for the reasons assigned, is extremely brittle. Neither does the chick always keep its head under its wing, so as to be thereby prevented from breaking the shell, but only when it sleeps or has died. For the creature wakes at intervals and scrapes, and kicks, and struggles, pressing against the shell, tearing the investing membranes and chirps (that this is done whilst petitioning for assistance I willingly concede), all of which things may readily be heard by any one who will use his ears. And the hen, listening attentively, when she hears the chirping deep within the egg, does not break the shell, but she turns the egg with her feet, and gives the chick within another and a more commodious position. But there is no occasion to suppose that the chick by his chirping informs his mother of the propriety of breaking the shell, or seeks deliverance from it; for very frequently for two days before the exclusion you may hear the chick chirping within the shell. Neither is the mother when she turns the egg looking for the proper place to break it; but as the child when uncomfortably laid in his cradle is restless and whimpers and cries, and his fond mother turns him this way and that, and rocks him till he is composed again, so does the hen when she hears the chick restless and chirping within the egg, and feels it, when hatched, moving uneasily about in the nest, immediately raise herself and observe that she is not pressing upon it with her weight, or keeping it too warm, or the like, and then with her bill and her feet she moves and turns the egg until the chick within is again at its ease and quiet."

This extract shows that here, as in all Harvey's work there was a union of common sense, observation, and experiment which enabled him to overturn without any unkindly feeling the cherished teachings of his predecessors and contemporaries.

When it was necessary he did not hesitate to experiment upon himself, for he says : " I have myself, for experiment's sake, occasionally pricked my hand with a clean needle, and then having rubbed the same needle on the teeth of a spider, I have pricked my hand in another place. I could not by my simple sensation perceive any difference between the two punctures : nevertheless there was a capacity in the skin to distinguish the one from the other ; for the part pricked by the envenomed needle immediately contracted into a tubercle, and by and by became red, hot, and inflamed, as if it collected and girded itself up for a contest with the poison for its overthrow."

The seventy-first essay of the treatise of Development is a good example of the mystic or philosophical side of Harvey's character. The essay is entitled " Of the innate Heat." It begins, " As frequent mention is made in the preceding pages of the calidum innatum or innate heat, I have determined to say a few words here, by way of dessert, both on that subject and on the humidum primigenium or radical moisture, to which I am all the more inclined because I observe that many pride themselves upon the use of these terms without, as I apprehend, rightly understanding their meaning. There is, in fact, no occasion for searching after spirits foreign to or distinct from the blood ; to evoke heat from another source ; to bring gods upon the scene, and to encumber philosophy with any fanciful conceits. What we are wont to derive from the stars is in truth produced at home. The blood is the only calidum innatum or first engendered animal heat."

Harvey then proceeds to examine the evidence for a spirit different from the innate heat, of celestial origin and nature, a body of perfect simplicity, most subtle, attenuated, mobile, rapid, lucid, ethereal, participant in the qualities of the quintessence. Of this spirit Harvey confesses that " we, for our own parts, who use our simple senses in studying natural things, have been unable anywhere to find anything of the sort. Neither are there any cavities for the production and preservation of such spirits, either in fact or presumed by their authors."

Harvey then discusses at some length the Aristotelian and scholastic views of the word "spirit" and "vital principle," and in the end arrives at the conclusion that "the blood, by reason of its admirable properties and powers, is 'spirit.' It is also celestial; for nature, the soul, that which answers to the essence of the stars is the inmate of the spirit, in other words, it is something analogous to heaven, the instrument of heaven, vicarious of heaven. . . . The blood, too, is the animal heat in so far namely as it is governed in its actions by the soul; for it is celestial as subservient to heaven, and divine because it is the instrument of God the great and good."

Harvey next attacks the doctrine of those who maintained that nothing composed of the elements can show powers superior to the forces exercised by these unless they at the same time partake of some other and more divine body, and on this ground conceive the spirits they evoke as constituted partly of the elements, partly of a certain ethereal and celestial substance. He observes very pertinently in opposition to such a train of reasoning : "In the first place you will scarcely find any elementary body which in acting does not exceed its proper powers; air and water, the winds and the ocean, when they waft navies to either

India and round this globe, and often by opposite
courses, when they grind, bake, dig, pump, saw
timber, sustain fire, support some things, overwhelm
others, and suffice for an infinite variety of other and
most admirable offices—who shall say that they do
not surpass the power of the elements? In like
manner what does not fire accomplish? In the kitchen,
in the furnace, in the laboratory, softening, hardening,
melting, subliming, changing, in an infinite variety of
ways! What shall we say of it when we see iron
itself produced by its agency?—iron 'that breaks the
stubborn soil and shakes the earth with war'! Iron
that in the magnet (to which Thales therefore ascribed
a soul) attracts other iron, 'subdues all other things
and seeks besides I know not what inane,' as Pliny
says; for the steel needle only rubbed with the lode-
stone still steadily points to the great cardinal points;
and when our clocks constantly indicate the hours of
the day and night, shall we not admit that all of these
partake of something else, and that of a more divine
nature than the elements? And if in the domain and
rule of nature so many excellent operations are daily
effected, surpassing the powers of the things themselves, what shall we not think possible within the
pale and regimen of nature, of which all art is but

imitation ? And if, as ministers of man, they effect such admirable ends, what I ask may we not expect of them, when they are instruments in the hand of God ?

"We must therefore make the distinction and say, that whilst no primary agent or prime efficient produces effects beyond its powers, every instrumental agent may exceed its own proper powers in action ; for it acts not merely by its own virtue but by the virtue of a superior efficient. . . .

Since the blood acts, then, with forces superior to the forces of the elements, and exerts its influence through these forces or virtues and is the instrument of the Great Workman, no one can ever sufficiently extol its admirable, its divine faculties.

"In the first place and especially, it is possessed by a soul which is not only vegetative, but sensitive and motive also. It penetrates everywhere and is ubiquitous; abstracted, the soul or the life too is gone, so that the blood does not seem to differ in any respect from the soul or the life itself (anima) ; at all events it is to be regarded as the substance whose act is the soul or the life. Such, I say, is the soul, which is neither wholly corporeal nor yet wholly incorporeal ; which is derived in part from abroad and is partly produced at home; which in one way is part of the body, but in another is the beginning and cause of all that is contained in the animal body, viz., nutrition, sense, and motion, and consequently of life and death alike; for whatever is nourished, is itself vivified, and *vice versâ*. In like manner that which is abundantly nourished increases; what is not sufficiently supplied shrinks; what is perfectly nourished preserves its health; what is not perfectly nourished falls into disease. The blood therefore, even as the soul, is to be regarded as the cause and author of youth and old age, of sleep and waking, and also of respiration. All the more and especially as the first instrument in natural things contains the internal moving cause within itself. It therefore comes to the same thing, whether we say that the soul and the blood, or the blood with the soul, or the soul with the blood performs all the acts in the animal organism." A lame and impotent conclusion which does not advance our knowledge, though perhaps it was the most plausible that could be drawn from the premisses at Harvey's command. Indeed he was himself dissatisfied with his conception of the vital principle, for in another essay after a discussion to show that the egg is not the product of the body of the hen, but is a result of the vital principle, he turns away from the subject with evident relief to more profitable subjects, and with the words "Leaving points that are doubtful and disquisitions bearing upon the general question, we now approach more definite and obvious matters."

The ideas then prevalent in physical science led him in like manner to spend much time and thought upon the unprofitable subject of the primigenial moisture, and with these speculations the treatise on development comes to an abrupt end.

The whole essay is an interesting one. It shows us the range of Harvey's mind filled with the knowledge of ancient philosophy, but animated by the experimental spirit of modern science. All that the work contains of observation and experiment is valuable, for Harvey had made use of his uncommon opportunities to acquire a knowledge, such as is usually possessed only by huntsmen and gamekeepers, and has very rarely been attained by a man of science. Harvey's knowledge, as shown in this treatise, may be compared to that shown by Darwin in his "Variation of Animals and Plants under Domestication." Harvey tries to explain his observations in the terms of an existing philosophy, while Darwin uses his facts to establish an original hypothesis of his own. We have so

completely outlived the age of the schoolmen that
it is difficult for us to recognise the bondage endured
by so great a mind as Harvey's until we consider it in
the light of Darwin's work. Then we recognise that
the theoretical disquisitions in the treatises on development are not so foreign to the true nature of Harvey
as they appear to be at first sight. They are in reality
an illustration of the profound influence of the prevalent
thought of a period upon every contemporary mind,
and show that the most thoughtful and original are
not always the least affected.

We thus take leave of one of the master minds of
the seventeenth century. Harvey's osteological lecture
has not yet been found, and many of his investigations
in comparative anatomy are still wanting. But there
is a possibility that his papers and books were only
dispersed, and were not destroyed at the pillage of his
lodgings in Whitehall. Some of the wreckage is still
cast up from time to time, and we may hope that more
may yet be found. So recently as 1888 Dr. Norman
Moore recognised thirty-five lines of Harvey's handwriting on a blank page at the end of the British
Museum copy of Goulston's edition of Galen's
"Opuscula Varia." Here, as in all the other manuscripts, the peculiarities of Harvey's writing are too

distinct to leave any doubt of the authorship. Every fragment of his work is interesting, and even in these few lines we seem to learn his opinion of artificial exterior elevation as opposed to the genuine exaltation of worth or learning, for against a passage in which Galen prefers learning to rank, Harvey has written "wooden leggs." A fitting testimony from one who, though he had spent the greater part of his life at court, was yet the foremost thinker of his age.

FINIS.

APPENDIX

APPENDIX

AUTHORITIES

CHAPTER I.

"The Genealogy of the Family of Harvey, compiled from Original Sources," by W. J. Harvey, Esq., F.S.A., Scotland, in the "Misc. Geneal. and Herald." Second Series, 1888–9, vol. iii. pp. 329, 362, 381.

Loftie's "History of London," ed. ii., vol. i.

Willis' "William Harvey," London, 1878.

Fuller's "Worthies of England," folio, 1662.

Sir James Paget's "Records of Harvey," London, (reprinted) 1887, by the kind permission of Sir James Paget, Bart., F.R.S.

Walpole's Works, Cunningham's ed. vol. vii., p. 329.

CHAPTER II.

Prof. Montague Burrows' "Cinque Ports" (Historic Towns), 1888.

Prof. George Darwin's " Monuments to Cambridge Men at the University of Padua." Publications of the Cambridge Antiquarian Society, vol. viii., 1895, pp. 337–347.

Andrich's " De natione Anglica," Padua, 1892.

Rashdall's " The Universities of Europe in the Middle Ages," Oxford, 1895.

The Harveian Orations of Dr. Barclay, Dr. Ogle, Dr. Johnson, Dr. Charles West, Dr. Pollock, and Dr. Pye-Smith.

Dr. Munk's " Roll of the College of Physicians," ed. ii.

Dr. Moore's Life of Harvey in the " Dictionary of National Biography."

Register of Marriage Licenses granted by the Bishop of London—Harleian Society's publications.

Sir James Paget's " Records of Harvey."

Harvey's Works—Sydenham Soc. Ed., London, 1847.

Information given by Prof. Carlo Ferraris, the Rector magnificus, and by Dr. Gerardi, the Librarian of the University of Padua, at the request of Prof. Villari and Prof. George Darwin, F.R.S.

CHAPTER III.

South's " Memorials of the Craft of Surgery," Messrs. Cassell, 1886.

Young's " Annals of the Barber Surgeons' Company."

Holingshed's Chronicle.

Alexander Reid's " Manual of Anatomy."

APPENDIX

The Harveian Orations of Sir George Paget, Sir E. H. Sieveking, Dr. Ogle, Dr. Charles West, Dr. Chambers, Dr. Johnson, Dr. Pavy, and Dr. Church.

Harvey's MS. Notes, Messrs. Churchill, London, 1886.

CHAPTER IV.

Calendar of State Papers—Domestic Series.

Aubrey's "Lives of Eminent Persons," London, 1813.

Munk's "Roll of the College of Physicians."

Munk's "Notæ Harveianæ," St. Bartholomew's Hospital Reports, vol. xxiii.

Wadd's "Mems., Maxims, and Memoirs."

Sir James Paget's "Records of Harvey."

Dr. Norman Moore's Life of Harvey in the "Dictionary of National Biography."

Mackay's "Memoirs of Extraordinary Popular Delusions."

Upham's "History of Witchcraft and Salem Village."

Young's "Annals of the Barber Surgeons' Company."

CHAPTER V.

Munk's "Notæ Harveianæ."

Gardiner's "History of the Great Civil War."

Aveling's "Memorials of Harvey," Messrs. Churchill, 1875.

Highmore's "Corporis Humani Disquisitio anatomica," folio, 1651.

APPENDIX

Aubrey's Lives of Eminent Persons.

Munk's " Roll of the College of Physicians."

Brodrick's " Memorials of Merton College," Oxford Historical Society.

Wood's " Life and Times," Oxford Historical Society's Edition.

The Harveian Orations of Dr. Rolleston and Dr. Andrew.

CHAPTER VI.

Willis' " William Harvey."

Wood's " Athenae Oxoniensis," Edition 1721

Aubrey's Lives of Eminent Persons.

MacMichael's Life of Harvey in " Lives of British Physicians."

Munk's " Notæ Harveianæ " and " Roll of the College of Physicians."

Harvey's Works—Sydenham Society's Edition.

Howell's " Epistolæ Ho-Elianæ," Ed., J. Jacobs, 1889.

Sir George Paget's " Account of an unpublished Manuscript of Harvey," London, 1850.

The Lancet, vol. ii., 1878, p. 176, and vol. ii., 1883, p. 706.

CHAPTER IX.

Brooks, W. K., " William Harvey as an Embryologist," *Johns Hopkins Hospital Bulletin*, vol. viii., p. 167.

Harvey's Notes on Galen, *The Athenæum*, October, 1888, No. 3180, p. 452.

INDEX

A

Alston, Dr., 157

Ameius Gulielmus, 18

Anatomical demonstrations, 41–46; method of conducting, 57–60; lectures, cost of, 45, 46; teaching of Reid compared with that of Harvey, 232–237; works of Harvey, 188

Anatomy, early teaching of, 39; study of, at Cambridge, 13; value of comparative, 201

Andrewes, Dr., 88, 90, 91, 97, 98, 104, 232

Andrich, Dr., 18, 27

Anecdotes of Eliab Harvey, 8; William Harvey, 144–145; Sir Charles Scarborough, 142

Appearance of Harvey, 52

Apothecaries' opinions of Harvey's prescriptions, 74; visitations of, 75–79

Aristotle, capillamenta of, 213; Harvey's opinion of, 68, 72

Armorial bearings of the Harvey family, 2

Art, Harvey an authority on, 115

Arteries, course of blood in, 213

Artistarum universitas, 16, 27

Arundel, Earl of, 111

Aubrey's first recollection of Harvey, 130; Harvey's advice to, 146

Auricle, movement of, 200

Autograph of Harvey in de Glarges' album, 123

Aveling, Dr., 83

Aylesford, Earls of, their relationship to Harvey, 7

271

INDEX

INDEX

The Gresham Press
UNWIN BROTHERS,
WOKING AND LONDON.

www.ingramcontent.com/pod-product-compliance
Lightning Source LLC
Chambersburg PA
CBHW020846020726
47497CB00005B/1284

* 9 7 8 3 3 3 7 4 2 4 7 5 6 *